KINDRED
Spirits

CELEBRATING ANGELS, MYSTICS & MIRACLES

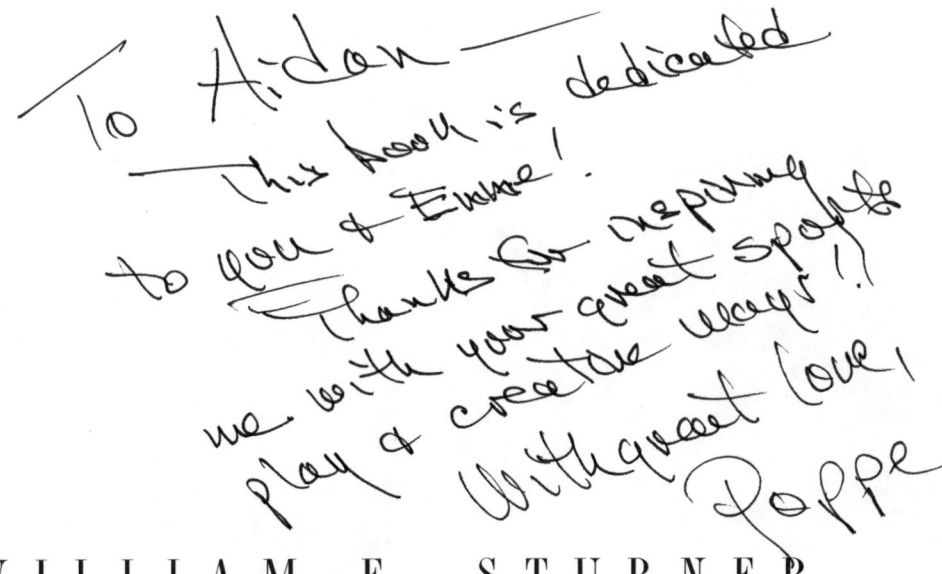

To Aidan —
This book is dedicated
to you & Emme!
Thanks for inspiring
us with your great spirit &
play & creative ways!!
With great love,
Poppe

April, 2011

W I L L I A M   F .   S T U R N E R

Other Books by William F. Sturner

BIOGRAPHICAL

Love Loops: A Divorced Father's Personal Journey (1983)

CREATIVITY

AHA: Creating Each Day with Insight and Daring (2000)

LEADERSHIP AND ORGANIZATIONAL CHANGE

Action Planning (1974)

Impact: Transforming Your Organization (1993)

Superb Leadership (1997)

MYTHIC SPIRIT TALES

The Three-Legged Deer: Exploring the Miracles of Nature (2010)

THE PSYCHOLOGY OF RISK AND CHANGE

Calculated Risk: Strategies for Managing Change (1990)

Risking Change: Ending and Beginnings (1987)

SPIRITUAL COMMENTARY

Mystic in the Marketplace: A Spiritual Journey (1994)

The Creative Impulse: A Jungian Approach to Genesis (1998)

Other Dimensions

East Aurora, New York

Presenting

Mythic Spirit-Tales, and

Spiritual Commentary

For the Childlike,

the Curious,

the Loving

and the Spiritually Inclined

Dedicated

TO AIDAN AND EMME

Aidan, a first-rate hockey and lacrosse player,

and the master of many disguises.

Emme, the lover of doggies,

swimming and everything she encounters.

Both are particularly special

because they are

also two of the brightest,

most adventurous

and most endearing

grandchildren

in the cosmos

In Appreciation

So much depends on who you meet, brush against, encounter - hang around with. So much also depends on who appears at opportune times and then periodically weaves in and out of your life. And so much depends on the chemistry, on the type of energy such people infuse into your life. The reason for the magical 'connect' may vary person to person, and may never be clearly defined. But you just know someone special has entered your life - bringing a certain joie de vie, an insightful slant on life, a graceful way of living, or an uncanny ability to create and express a bit of beauty and love you may have missed otherwise.

Usually these significant others are not even aware of how positively they affect you; as far as they know, they are just being who they are.

I have been fortunate enough, for example, to have a few teachers whose words and actions effected me deeply. Mrs. Mangan (I never learned her first name; it may have been Eleanor) was the librarian at Evander Childs High School in the Bronx in the fifties; Edward A. Walsh was the faculty overseer for the Fordham College Ram, the campus newspaper when I was a co-sports editor in 1956-57; and Robert Pollock was a Philosophy professor at Fordham University when I returned there for graduate work in the sixties.

Then there is the recurring camaraderie of many 'old' friends. I hesitate to mention individual names because I don't want to leave someone out who really should be at the top of the list. I will at least use a very high bar – including only those special friendships that go back at least thirty-five years. (Thirty-five years? Yes – thirty-five years!)

Easily leaping over even that high bar are my dear friends Linda Ward, Gus Jacacci, Joe Murphy, Mel and Dee Cherno, Matteo Catullo, Bill and Phyllis Marshall, John Hornecker, Lillian Maresch, Jean Chatigny, Lee Dunne, Jean Côté, John Sedgwick, Len Finkelstein, John Broomfield and Jo Imlay, Doug and Judy Reid, Joette Field, René Bernèche and Sid and Bea Parnes — none of whom I now see very often but all of whom I still treasure despite the geographic distance.

And, of course, there are my daughters, Kelly Ostrowski and Kristin Linthwaite, both of whom I have also known and prized for at least thirty-five years. Courage, fortitude, focus and love describe their essence — a composite contribution they create in abundance every week of the year. What more could a parent ask than to knowingly model his life on the perspectives created by his own children.

Most Immediately

If I was to list - and thus thank — all the people who have and continue to bring insight and ease into my life I would need another volume. Ah — a good idea: a book just to list and thank friends and colleagues. That I could write easily.

But most immediately, however, I want to extend my special thanks to Judy Hooper — sheep farmer, Ph.D. chemist, Jungian analyst-in-training and delightful friend - who brought a keen eye and insightful reading to each of the three stories in this book.

Foundational

I also want to acknowledge the foundational figures whose actions and writings have inspired me - and millions of others — to delight in the mysterious and the mystical and thus the spiritual.

Gandhi's phrase: "I don't have a resume. My life is my resume" - says it all. And so it has been as well for Martin Luther King, Mother Theresa, Nelson Mandela and the Dalai Lama.

The eyes and inner ears of Thomas Merton were so attuned to spiritual realities that his writings continue to transport me to realms I cannot easily access on my own.

Professor Robert Pollock, mentioned above, surely had a direct link with Prime Source and the angelic realms. His weekly lectures contained the most inspired insights into the workings of spirit that any of us who crowded into his lecture room were ever likely to hear. He was as stunning as he was inspirational – so much so that not one of the iconoclasts who gathered for his three-hour lecture each week ever wanted to interrupt him. Questions came later – at the end of lecture or in the hallway. But once he started, the setting literally became sacred space - and you did little but listen, and take notes and hold your breath.

Foremost among the works that have inspired my appreciation of the spiritual nature of the universe are the writings of psychologist C.G. Jung and J.R.R. Tolkien, and the art of Wassily Kandinsky and the Renaissance triumvirate of Leonardo, Raphael and Michelangelo. Books I return to again and again include *The Way of Zen* by Alan Watts, *The Little Prince* by Antoine Exupéry, *The Prophet* by Kahlil Gibran, *Mr. Blue* by Myles Connolly, and JRR Tolkien's *The Hobbit*.

These - and many others – continue to evoke a vivid awareness of Spirit's presence everywhere and in everyone. And the workings of Spirit are revealed most poignantly - and frequently - in and through the natural processes of ordinary living. The mythic tales highlighted in this volume are thus drawn from a series of everyday experiences of extraordinary realities.

A Trilogy of Spiritual Tales

The story of how four young adults honor their experiences of the spiritual realm: out-of- body travel, visionary dreams, detecting the divinity embedded in nature, and receiving angelic help in time of need. The foursome share their encounters and then collaborate to encourage others to affirm their own spiritual experiences.

Six unique Souls follow a mysterious 'light' into a well-lit stadium only to discover their mortal lives have ended. Now back in the realm of Pure Spirit, they tour the facilities of 'heaven' and 'hell', undergo a series of heart-warming Life Reviews, and even consult the Akashic Records on past and future life choices. Enlightened by angels and chastened by re-enactments of their lives, all six choose to return to Earth as newborns. Their mission: to create – this time - as much zest and compassion aspossible.

A fascinating cast of characters becomes one big, cooperative and cosmic team. There are humans, who with the aid of angels, restructure their lives and commit to helping others. There are Guardian Angels in Training who finally learn how to listen to their human charges. And last, there's the radiance of Archangels Gabriel, Raphael and Michael — who use their awesome powers to 'enlighten' both angels and humans, and even deter any who dare challenge what God Herself has blessed.

The Essential Introduction

If you were looking for Spirit – I mean a direct encounter with spiritual reality – where would you go or what would you do?

We are not talking here about a theory or a concept of God, or even participating in a revered religious ritual, hearing a glorious sermon or having a reading with a first rate channel or kabalistic astrologer. The testimonies presented here, although embedded in fictional details, are actually reenactments of insights into and encounters with 'the other side'.

Some may refer to such involvements as extraordinary. But tapping into our Soul's spiritual powers, and using them to access the other spiritual dimensions of our reality, have - for generations - been everyday experiences for a great number of people. One need only consult the sacred books of every spiritual tradition and the remarkable testimonies offered by the mystics of every religion to find repeated references to all the experiences described here.

Our three stories also do not involve any intermediaries - like a minister, a séance convener or even a ouija board. What's described here are direct and personal encounters – involving everyday people who either have an out-of-body experience, enter into the eternal moment of 'now, reenter the realm of Pure Spirit following the death of their bodies, or interact with an array of angels, Guardian Angels and Archangels.

Gauging from *our first story*, **Kindred Spirits**, any of us could have an out-of-body experience. The immortal Soul – unhindered by the body's density when it sleeps – can easily move through the multiple dimensions of the *spiritual universe* – and usually does so to provide aid to those in need. Vivid dreams can also reveal the true nature of the cos-

mos. And certainly a deep appreciation of beauty – as in the magnificence of the center of flower or the face of the newborn – can usher in an intense experience of living in the timeless or eternal dimension of *now*.

A very different set of **Choices** is presented *in our second story*. Here a set of six delightful characters find they have returned to the realm of Pure Spirit following their mortal death. Initially their placements mirror their expectations – with *heaven, hell* and even *purgatory* becoming temporary realities. But spiritual guides help each Soul review and learn from their earlier stays on Earth. And the insights gained encourage each of them to choose love and joy as the major themes of their next re-incarnation on Earth.

The third story - **Angels at Work** - features a fascinating cast of characters. Humans restructure their lives after having profound interactions with visiting angels. Guardian Angels in Training learn how to interact with their human charges. And the infamous trio of Archangels Gabriel, Raphael and Michael use their respective teaching, healing and protective skills to elevate here, enlighten there and safeguard the loving - everywhere.

Such are the varied ways of cultivating direct contact with the spiritual realm. In fact, the kinds of supra-ordinary contacts described here would be common experiences for all if – being true to our mystical and religious traditions – we realized we are integral parts of a spiritual universe, that God and the angelic hierarchy are ever-present, and that each of us is nothing less than an immortal Soul having an earthly experience.

It unfortunate that it takes shedding the mortal body for many to realize the sacred nature of our soulful identity. Those of us in the midst of completing an incarnation on Earth, however, are as free as the characters in our stories to lay full claim to our spiritual heritage: we all still have plenty of time to cultivate our momentous extra-sensory capacities, and both seize on - and give thanks for - the dazzling empowerments that are part and parcel of our everyday identity.

Kindred Spirits

Affirming Our Encounters With Spirit

The story of how four young adults

discover their spiritual identities –

one affirms his out-of- body experiences,

another honors the cosmic images in her dreams,

a third accesses the eternal 'now' present in nature,

and the fourth describes the angelic assistance received in time of
need.

The foursome meet and share,

solidify their friendship as 'Kindred Spirits',

then found a website that encourages others

to share their experiences of Spirit.

Must Record It

Sam sat at his desk for a long time – thinking about the notes he had scribbled during the night. He woke suddenly from a dream around three a.m., quickly reaching for the pad next to his bed to record whatever he could remember.

Come morning, he was awakened by the sound of chimes – something that had happened before and always as a marker of a special

event. He checked the clock and was not surprised to find it was still a half-hour before the alarm was set to go off. Awake, he sat up, rubbed his eyes - then suddenly reached for his notes. What do they say? They were too hard to decipher: too fragmented, blurry and jumbled for a quick translation.

Brushing the covers aside, Sam fiddled with and finally got his feet into his slippers, stopped to pee, washed his hands, and found himself at the sink brushing his teeth. Then he grabbed his notes, negotiated the first turn of the banister, next the landing, stumbled down the remaining stairs, swerved to enter his study, finally sitting down on the corner of the chair and turning on his computer.

'Trav'l' was one word and another looked like, yes it was, 'space'. 'Jufiter' - he now recalled – referred to 'Jupiter' and 'dist' and 'blue dot' were linked to the scribble of 'eart'. At the bottom of the page were jottings that looked like the words 'closer, clods, h2o.' It was not the whole story but it was now enough for him to recreate the experience.

"Must record the specifics now – as soon as I can – before I lose them," he kept muttering to himself. He patched the sequence together as best he could, then dashed upstairs to get dressed, and dashed back down again to add a few more details. It was now 7:23. "Wow," was all he kept saying to himself. "Wow."

Share With Care

Sam had little time to think about his dream for the rest of the morning: he had a meeting with the publisher, another with the business department and then a much longer one with his arts and cultures staff. All the options for next week's edition had been aired and Sam had selected and assigned the four lead stories and seven others. There was no sense tackling the e-mail correspondence right now. Best take a short break and a quick walk around the square.

Scott, the paper's photographer, and Roy, the paper's senior reporter, walked with him. "Good meeting," "lovely day," "not bad: a pre-Broadway show in town", and "good report on the museum"– were among the comments shared in rapid succession.

"You are quiet today, Sam 'ol boy," said Roy. "Not like you."

"Oh – was just thinking – had a wild and wonderful dream last night."

"Ah-oh," laughed Scott. "Another one of your forays into inner – or should we say – outer space?"

"Or maybe one of the angels left its pedestal in some chapel and came to visit you," added Roy. "Remember: a good editor has to remain grounded - his mind on this week, this town, *this* world."

Sam smiled – sighed – then grimaced. His comments a month ago about sensing angels in our midst – "angels you don't necessarily see but which could be sensed" – did not go over well when the staff gathered for a few beers and a TGIF celebration. Figuring it was as good a time as ever - when the armor might be off and people's guards down - he asked if anyone had ever been visited by an angel. "Oh do tell," was the general response. They heard him all right – to his continuing regret.

There was no beer in sight that afternoon as the threesome strolled through downtown, yet Sam doubted if sobriety would induce an open mind any more than the alcohol had. Best not take another chance; it would spare him another round of ridicule.

"No - just a wonderful dream that made me feel good," said Sam finally. "Maybe some day I will attempt again to share more, but certainly not with valueless freeloaders like you. Go to church but not believe in angels? You ought to be excommunicated," Sam taunted. "To the fires of Hell with both of you," he said as he challenged his colleagues to a quick jog back to the office.

More Than a Dream

"You look puzzled but delighted. What's going on?" asked Rhonda, her eyebrows raised dramatically over her enlarged eyes - her chin and neck crooked forward.

"I hesitate to talk about it," said Sam. "I trust you not to dismiss it, but still it's difficult talking about something so audacious and by traditional standards pretty silly and impossible."

He started to say more but then just smiled... and sat silently, trying to escape his friend's glances.

She sighed deeply, scratched her head, sang a few notes of a popular song, and then slowly reached in Sam's direction, curled her fingers toward her in alternating circles – and encouraged Sam to say more. They had not known each other very long but when they met two months ago at a party, it was like old-home week: for Sam – a woman he could talk to; for Rhonda, a warm and bright man she could respect. They both assumed romance could develop in the future – if that is what seemed right. In the meantime, a friend is what both needed most, and fast-and- trusted-friends is what they had become.

"Okay, okay, okay. Actually it will be a relief finally to talk about it. It has happened many times. This time it was really powerful and I can't shake it or ignore it. Ready?"

"Ready."

"I woke up this morning to a faint sound of chimes: gentle, easy, soothing – which is usually what I hear when coming out of a certain kind of dream, or should I say – the kind of 'experience' - I had again last night. I had woken up earlier to record what I remembered of the dream on the pad I keep near my bed. Then I apparently drifted back into the same dream – and so this morning I also recalled additional material. This kind of thing has happened to me a lot in the last year. This time it was extra vivid – like I was really there. I take that back: it was not *like* I was there. I *was* there."

"Yes, yes, and….?" said Rhonda taking a deep breath.

"Well, I was flying. I was flying in deep outer space. I was zooming through space. Lights, stars - glittered in front of me. Some seemed very close. Others were merely tiny dots in the distance. It was totally silent except for the rippling sound I made as I flew through the air."

"Lights, stars - glittered in front of me. Some seemed very close. Others were merely tiny dots in the distance. It was totally silent except for the rippling sound I made as I flew through the air."

"Fly-ing th-rough the air," Rhonda repeated slowly.

"Yes – literally flying through space itself," said Sam with an extra sense of gusto.

"It was incredible, he continued, "especially when I rounded an enormous planet - or whatever it was - that was so large and opaque that it blotted out all sparkling lights I saw earlier. The name of Jupiter kept coming through. When I emerged on its far side, I was startled by the sight of a tiny, luminous blue light blinking far in the distance."

Rhonda put up her hand, reached for Sam's glass of water, took a few swallows, then wetting her fingers, sprayed flicks of water on Sam's face.

"Are you going to listen, or what?" asked Sam.

"Yes, yes, sorry – it is just so remarkable. Forgive me. You know me: I get nervous when things get serious. Please, please – continue. I'm with you."

"So there I was," said Sam after a long breath, "there I was zooming through space – not pushed or propelled – but as if drawn by a powerful magnet, literally being pulled back toward the Earth, that blue dot growing increasingly larger and larger until it was all I could see."

He put his head in his hands, and choking back tears, told his friend that then "whole continents came into view. I was stunned. I was descending onto earth."

Stunned, Puzzled and Delighted

"My water, right?" said Sam as he reached for the glass.

"Take your time," said Rhonda, as she placed her hand on his.

"Then…then, all I could see were mixtures - swirls of water and strips of land, whirling together, rapid, rapid, until everything became a massive blur, until I woke up, suddenly – in my own bed."

He was silent for a moment as his breathing slowed.

Finally he said: "When I woke up, as I told you, I first heard the faint chime of bells. That happens every time I have one of my out-of-body experiences – apparently signaling my Soul's return from a night's travel. It is the signal, it seems, that I – as a Soul - have eased myself back into my body, and am ready to resume my ordinary earthly existence."

Moments passed in relative silence – followed by a few sighs on either side, then rhythmic breathing reduced the clamor of the restaurant to faint white noise.

"I laid very still for several seconds," Sam finally said, "fully awake but confused, filled with energy - my body quivering internally – yet I was also feeling numb. I was stunned and puzzled and delighted – all at the same time. I remember saying 'wow' – over and over again. This has happened many times before but never this powerful, this vivid, this real. Suddenly I realized I needed to record it all – so I grabbed my notes and rushed downstairs to my computer."

They just looked at each other. "Thank you," said Rhonda. "Thank you, thank you. I feel privileged. And I believe you, Sam – totally."

"Yes," uttered Sam. "Thanks. It feels so good to share what I know sounds wild - but which is as true as our sitting here. I really appreciate your listening…and your acceptance. I have been meaning to share my experiences with you for some time – and this time, with the dream being as intense as it was, well - the time seemed right."

Rhonda – wide-eyed and smiling, just shook her head in assent. "I'm glad," she said. "That also makes me feel really good."

"One more thing," said Sam, interrupting the long silence. "I know I said it before but I want to say it again. Although what happened occurred in a dream, I know it happened to me. I know it as 'my experience' – not just a dream about some mysterious occurrence. I have long known that our Souls travel freely at night – and do all sorts of things -

like helping others and traveling to distant places to obtain advice and instruction."

"So the key for me,' he said with emphasis, "is that it was me – the body-spirit - who had a dream, and it was me – the *spirit-body* – that had the experience. The dream just recorded the experience – like a videotape. So in one sense, given conventional reality, I know it is as crazy as all get-out. But it is all true, absolutely true - nonetheless! Wow! Gawd, but I feel good!"

Multiple Glimpses

Rhonda was quiet and thoughtful. She cupped her chin in her hands, and in looking up, finally said, "Sam – 'wow' - is right. That's incredible."

"Astounding," she added. "It makes me recall the similar kinds of experience I've also had, different from yours, but equally mysterious and wild."

"But before I reveal my encounters, tell me – are your experiences confined to dreams or have other things happened to you as well?" she inquired.

"I've had lots of dreams of out-of-body experiences – some bits and pieces, some longer – but none as full and complete as the one I just described," Sam responded.

"But my experience of what I call 'the other side' has not just been confined to dreams … or night dreaming. I have all sorts of encounters, big and little ones – what I call 'glimpses' – fleeting experiences, daydreams and strong intuitions, even sensing someone or something is present, standing close to me, like an angel – something obviously from another world – but I always sense it is a loving and spiritual presence."

"It is all strange – but none of it is scary," he continued. "Sometimes I have realizations or flashes of insight. Other times I resonate with a feeling. Another experience may simply register as an 'awareness'. I don't know what else to call them: they are something I sense or glimpse – then they're gone in a flash. They come and go – yet they all seem to be related and reinforce each other. And they all seem to come from the same or a similar source, namely, a spiritual world that is just beyond our ordinary reach but accessible to us … if we're open to it."

"That is what fascinates me most," said Rhonda, "is that you refer to each encounter – including your dream - as an 'experience' – not just an insight or an idea like some mental construct or sentimental feeling. You tell your stories as a direct participant, in which you are totally engaged, in which you are fully involved in that 'reality'. And each experience, if I hear you correctly, is a clue that literally affirms you as a spiritual being – or at least a person capable of extra-ordinary, extra-sensory experiences."

"Absolutely," said Sam.

"So take this recent dream, as an example," Rhonda continued. "You experience yourself in free flight, able to defy the usual restrictions of the body – implying that *you* are also distinct from your ordinary physical body. You are in essence saying, that during sleep, when you surrender your conscious boundaries - you shed the normal physical restrictions and live without or outside the normal boundaries."

"When you play it back to me, it gives me goose-bumps," said Sam. "Obviously there's a reason we're having lunch today. I knew you would understand. I just knew it."

Rhonda sighed. "Oh goodness. Unfortunately I have to get back to work. Boo. I definitely want to explore this 'other side' stuff some more: your take on it … *and mine*. So - tomorrow, here, twelve-noon sharp, our regular table – you, me – to be continued. Okay? Please I want to hear more – including your other dreams and your other experiences."

She grabbed her purse and knapsack, then added with emphasis: "I so want to share my stuff too. It is all wild and wonderful. Holy Mackerel. This is marvelous: both of us coming out of the spiritual closet in the same day. Oh my gawd, oh my gawd! Love you. Got to run. Tomorrow. Here. Noon. Don't forget. Soul-mapping! Yes!"

Kosmic Crystal

"Well", said Rhonda, with a broad smile and a deep sigh. "I have never told anyone about this, I mean the dream I had a few years ago that blew my mind. Like you, there is a lot of other stuff too – but this one particular dream is key to it all."

"It was particularly powerful," she continued, "because it confirmed and reinforced many other kinds of experience – motivating me to think of myself more and more, not just as Rhonda, but Rhonda who was first and foremost a Soul, who had taken on a body in order to accomplish some things here on Earth. Suddenly it all made sense. But I get ahead of myself. First the dream that unified it all."

"Initially, I did not know what to think of it – but I wrote it down because I just knew it was important. I have those journal notes with me. That original image has been amplified since by subsequent dreams that kept adding specifics – making it both fuller and more specific."

"Sounds like quite the drama," said Sam. "And the drawings? Do you have them too?"

"Yes – I will show them to you but first let me describe the central dream."

"Okay ... but I'm sorry: before your start, do you have a name or short headline description of the dream?"

"A ball of light," she said. "Now do you want to hear this or not?"

"Yes, yes, yes. Sor-ry."

"The essence of the image is always the same. At first, all I was able to remember was a gigantic sphere of light – rounded but blurry at the edges. And all points on this gigantic 'ball of light' were individual points within a whole. Thousands, millions of these points were already lit but I also had a sense that many others were waiting to be activated. That was it the first time around."

"Color?"

"Yes – white against a dark background – something that was not confirmed or evident to me until the dream occurred again six months later. Then I realized the image was composed of a gazillion white dots. The white lights were heavily clustered in the center so the center looked almost pure white. The entire image was filled with light or white dots but the intensity gradually diminished – and the outermost edges seemed only blurred with a shattering of dots."

"Do you know what it meant?" asked Sam.

"At the time I had no idea. All I knew was I was dazzled. Was this me and my brain, a symbol perhaps of all the cells finally waking up?" she said with a giggle. "Or was it a commentary on something bigger and deeper? That question was clarified a year or so later when the dream reappeared during my long illness – a really dark time, physically and mentally, causing me to doubt my role, my contribution... even my significance."

Multiple Dimensions

"I remember being awakened when the dream reoccurred. Like you, I remember becoming an active participant - like the pilgrim in that old medieval woodcut who lifts the curtain on the Earth's normal or assumed outer edge of its atmosphere and discovers it is only a part of a much larger, more complex and absolutely dazzling universe."

"I have since sought out that woodcut. I remember seeing it in a magazine - years ago. I finally found a reproduction of it in a book on *Astronomy* by a man named Camille Flammarion. It pictures a bedazzled pilgrim lifting a curtain on his everyday universe and discovering the huge cosmos that surrounds it. On the 'outer or fuller universe' are huge mountains, discs of light and even the wheels of God's throne as envisioned by Ezekiel."

"My dream, of course, was very different from Flammarion's depiction. But like that medieval woodcut, I too felt like I was lifting the cover of my or our assumed universe, and lo and behold - discovering a much larger - and in fact, gigantic cosmos - within which the earth and our Milky Way were mere dots."

"Subsequent dreams filled in the specifics – the ball of light becoming in my mind symbolic of our expanding physical universe. Equally incredible – if not more so – was the realization that this mass of lights depicted the billions of individual Souls that exists in the cosmos – one of whom was probably you flying through space on your way back to Earth!"

"But – of course," said Sam smiling.

"The fuller image of the universe that I subsequently experienced repeated the image I had seen in earlier dreams. Gradually, the layout and the meaning were clearer. I soon realized that each point depicted on and within the ball was actually an individual or unique cell or aspect within a giant organism. Each point of light was a spark or element in an ever-expanding crystal or diamond," said Rhonda.

"And, and" she quickly added with her hands up as Sam moved forward as if to ask a question– "each tiny facet – of Soul - expressed its own unique variation on life while being simultaneously related to all the other facets. Each point, cell, facet or Soul – or whatever they are called - thus contributed to and was an integral part of this cumulative kosmic presence."

"A bedazzled pilgrim lifting a curtain on his everyday universe and discovering the huge cosmos that surrounds it. On the 'outer or fuller universe' are huge mountains, discs of light and even the wheels of God's throne as envisioned by Ezekiel."

"Rhonda, Rhonda, Rhonda," said Sam in rapid succession. "Please let me play some of this back to you. I also need to ask a question or two - because I am getting lost."

"Of course, you're right. I'll slow down. Please play it back to me and ask anything your want. But then, realize, I also need to finish – 'cus there's more."

Back and forth they went, Sam asking questions and checking out what he thought he heard, Rhonda clarifying and sometimes adding a detail to her descriptions of her image.

"Okay?" Rhonda asked.

"Got it, so far. Thank you," said Sam.

"Now to the drawing," said Rhonda. "When I drew a picture of this dream image, which I now call 'a kosmic mandala', I allowed myself to follow my natural inclinations and my inspirations from the dreams. It is a play on what Carl Jung called the 'active imagination' – letting our unconscious imagination fill in and extend the details of an experience. The result in my case is this image of a crystal that has both an ever-deepening center and ever-expanding circumference."

A Vision of Unity

Rhonda then opened the drawing and spread it on the table. They were now sitting side by side.

"Now you ask, what does it mean?" she chuckled. "Well, I let a few days go by after completing the first draft. Then after recalling my dreams, I reviewed my notes and descriptions, studied both my original and my amplified drawings, re-read some portions of the Bible, and then scampered through the notes I had accumulated on the likes of Rudolf Steiner, Hillegard of Bingen, Giordano Bruno, Meister Eckhart and Madame Blavatsky – you know the spiritual masters that nobody in traditional circles likes to talk about - and I finally reached a few conclusions. I have written them down. Here goes."

"There are a number of issues that together form an integrated system," said Rhonda, pointing to various portions of her diagram as she explained the next, and the next aspect of what she called her 'grand realization'.

"One, the dream, the image - is a vision of the entire universe."

"The entire universe?" asked Sam with a quizzical look.

"Yes: our *en-tire and in-cred-ible uni-verse*," said Sally slowly and with emphasis.

"Two, I just knew that every tiny dot in my dream-image was a Soul, a living cell of the living organism that we know, physically, as the cosmos - and spiritually as Prime Source or God."

"Three, every dot or facet has a role to play in the grand illumination of the universe."

"Four, every dot or spark of light – those that merge into a continuous stream of light at the center of the globe as well as those at the margins – is an integral part in the unfolding of our ever expanding universe."

"Five, no point is better or of lesser importance than another. All points simply are, and are equal in their essence. Each one has the capacity to contribute or gift its light to others and in turn receive and reflect the light of others."

"You are blowing my mind," interjected Sam. "It holds together but it is hard to get my head around something so big, so cosmic, so unbelievable."

"Hey: be patient!" retorted Rhonda with a smile and a pat on Sam's head. "I have just two more, a sort of grand finale. Drum roll please…

"Six, each point, although equal in essence to all others, possesses certain distinctive qualities and occupies a distinct location. Thus no other point of light has its special radiance and no other can make its kind of unique contribution to the totality."

"And finally: number seven. The totality is a ball of light. And the entire circumference is aglow - like an enormous sun emitting rays of shimmering flares. It is perfectly centered and balanced – like a cosmic mandala - with all its power seeming to come from and return to its center. Yet it is expanding continuously, both inwardly toward greater and greater depth, and outwardly through ever-expanding degrees of breadth and height. In short, the ball of light is everything."

There was silence. Rhonda and Sam simply looked at each other.

"Oh my gawd, it's stunning. The whole thing: the dream, the drawing, the interpretation. Thank you, thank you," Sam said with great excitement. "I'm stunned," he added as he reached over to give Rhonda a hi-five, then a hug.

He then reached for her hand, exhaled heavily, and then, with an impish smile, he asked softly: "That's all? That's all you got?"

"That's it for now, wise guy," Rhonda responded with a giggle. "The other stuff – and there is lots of it - will be revealed at another time. But now, to celebrate things that are round, balanced and centered – I recommend we go crazy and order a super large pizza ...with everything on it. I'm starved."

Giving Thanks

"I love it," Sam continued. "Your story, your insight – is the ultimate in thinking big. It would drive Professor Jenkins – of my MBA class in Micro Economics - absolutely wild. It certainly is not conventional. By ordinary standards it is not 'rational'. But it is mystical all the way. All those spiritual writers of the past you have befriended would be delighted, would be so proud of you - and cheering you on."

Sam paused, then added: "I especially like it because it would apparently also include me and my - now - 'little' story of space travel in our local part of the cosmos."

Rhonda laughed, and squeezed his hand.

"But I need to be honest," said Sam. "Your experience of the nature of the universe, you insight into its workings, is so enormous and astounding that initially I had trouble understanding it no less agreeing with it. Frankly, I was – and am partially numb. But your total description – especially the drawings – put it all in perspective, making it all ring true in a mystical sense. I simply cannot thank you enough. It is gorgeous, horrendous, amazing – and I am so proud of you."

"The entire circumference is aglow - like an enormous sun emitting rays of shimmering flares. And the sphere is perfectly centered and balanced – like a cosmic mandala."

"Both of us — out of our spiritual closets," he continued, "whammo-slammo - onto center stage, glorious witnesses to a mystical universe, our testimonies so unconventional that we are sure to be viewed as weird by anyone who has not had a similar experience - or refuses to admit it."

"It *is* strange — and wonderful, isn't it" observed Rhonda. "And it feels so good to come up and out of the cellar, to no longer hide, to literally climb up the stairs into the full daylight and declare oneself - to at least one other person!"

Both brimmed with smiles and laughter - and then - suddenly - both were fighting off tears.

"Now that we have gone public before God and each other, can we risk going public with everyone?" said Sam.

"We can pick and choose — as we did with each other — and as it feels safe," came Rhonda's response. "Those with conventional religious beliefs might think we were crazy — although the mystics would surely understand and cheer us on. We just want to honor our experiences for what they are — apparent glimpses into a spiritual universe. And we'll share them with others - if and when that seems right."

"Let's celebrate," they laughingly said in unison.

"But, first," suggested Rhonda, "how about our just giving thanks with a moment of silence."

Everything and everyone else in the restaurant continued as usual: glasses clinked, dishes scrapped, laughter erupted, some people left and others arrived — the world rolled on as usual — as Sam and Rhonda choose to stop for a moment - and pay homage, to exactly what — was not clear. Perhaps their tribute was to a higher spirit, or the gift of a spiritual experience, or the bond that was obviously growing between them. Perhaps they were overwhelmed by all three energies converging at once. They looked across the table at each other, linked their hands - in layers - bowed their heads, and together murmured: "We give thanks."

One More Time – Once

Both sniffled and reached for tissues – laughing, leaning back, then coming forward again to hold hands again.

"Now, how about a quick walk in the park where we can at least celebrate with the animals and the flowers," said Rhonda shrugging her shoulders and laughing. "Surely they are among those who know all about this stuff."

"Let's do it," said Sam.

As they stood, reaching in pocket and purse to share the bill, they heard someone call softly to them – just off to the left.

"Excuse me," said a voice – then a face – from the table to the side of theirs. "Mind if I say hello. I hope you don't mind - but I happened to overheard bits of your conversation – you were so excited - you may have been talking louder than you intended. I apologize if I heard something I was not supposed to. But there was something about "a ball of light" and recently, a reference to "a spiritual universe.""

"Oh gawd," she said, putting her hand to her mouth. "I apologize. I think I may have overstepped my boundaries. Really. I'll go. I am really sorry."

Startled, Sam and Rhonda exchanged glances - then focused on the young woman in the bright yellow blouse.

"Its just," the woman started to say - when Rhonda reached over, touched her shoulder and encouraged her to stay.

"It's just that I have been trying to take risks lately - for what I believe in - and to just trust myself. Your comments, my reactions to the vibrations coming from your booth, it felt right to take a chance. You see I have a story too, a story that also proves to me that we live in a universe more strange and wonderful than any of us ever imagined."

Rhonda and Sam looked at each other - mouths half open, eyes wide open.

"Why... why, of course," they said. "No problem. Please join us. We are just going for a walk."

"Amazing", "thank you", "are you sure?"

"Yes, yes, yes, please" and "thank you, thank you"- were the words spoken more than once as the threesome negotiated the swinging doors.

Chance Connections

"I'm an artist," said Sally as she walked along the lake path with Sam and Rhonda. "I do flowers, scenes from nature – this, now – this lake and the flowering crab trees – are what attracts me most. Yet I love to paint all the seasons - the woodlands in snow, the fall colors. All aspects of nature energize and delight me."

"Well my story of 'our incredible universe' – as I think I heard one of you call it – involves a different medium than yours. Other things may be beckoning to you as well, but I understand your most profound experience – Rhonda - was with a dream. Well, mine comes through a set of everyday experiences – and most recently in and through my art."

Sam and Rhonda listened intently as Sally stopped to take out a sketchbook from her backpack.

"Here's a few examples," she said as she flipped through the book.

"I've not had an easy year. My mother died a year ago and then I lost my job – and even my relationship fell apart. I became desperately lonely - and despite my strong streak of independence and grounding in my parents' agnosticism – I finally gave in and asked God and the universe for help – help for everyday living as well as some sign that I or we were not alone. I was getting suicidal."

"Well," she continued, "things did not change immediately – like that same day – but they sure have changed ever since. Here I am going on and on. I am sorry. I hope you don't mind. I know we just met but our so-called chance meeting is just like my other chance encounters. They not only 'just happen' but also seem like they are meant to be."

"Please, Sally, we are anything but bored. And we also think there's no such thing as a chance encounter. If our meeting has some significance to you," said Rhonda looking at Sam who was nodding his head in agreement, "then please know it also has spiritual significance for us. An hour ago, the two of us were a pair of marbles – on the same plate – colliding, so to speak, but not really connecting in a substantive way. But things have changed a lot – at least I think so – since we told each other about our spiritual experiences."

"Right?" she asked Sam, with a soft jab to the arm.

"Absolutely," Sam replied with a hug and tender kiss on the side of her forehead.

"You overheard at least smidges of my story," said Rhonda, "and you are now sharing yours. So we are acquainted. Now let's see if we are knowingly connected in a deeper way. Please go on."

We Are Not Alone

"Well all I know," said Sally with a sigh of relief, "is that I'm sure our meeting was not simply by chance. I used to think that help from God came like a thunderbolt and everything would immediately be changed for the better. That would be nice but I now realize – is a bit too easy."

"Besides," said Sally laughing, "that would mean God would be doing all the work. Now I know that divine guidance comes in the form of little gifts which if seized upon lead to a series of others. The key is to follow the hints and invitations as they appear – as if they were left on a

trail for us to find. It is like the oxherding pictures in Zen Buddhism, if you know of them? None of the tracings are conclusive in themselves — but they progressively lead to a great insight and discovery."

"I like it," said Sam.

"I love it," said Rhonda. "And you've gotten us excited. So pl-ease tell us more – at your own pace, of course - but as quickly as you can," she added, giggling at her own excitement.

"Well, in no order of sequence, but just what stands out. My Mom had a favorite saying, "Keep trying." And there they were, those very words - underlined, mind you - in a magazine I just happened to pick up at a dentist's office. Then the night I was thinking of committing suicide, a 18-wheeler suddenly pulled in front of me on the highway, and there, scrawled in the cumulative grime - in letters that must have been two feet tall - were the words, 'Live, Please Live."

She paused.

"There's so much, so much. Once I asked for guidance while walking through a busy and noisy corridor of an airport. A moment later I stopped to switch my carry-on to the opposite shoulder and suddenly the white-noise of the airport stopped and I heard a voice say as audibly and distinctly as yours or mine: 'You are loved.' Then the noise level went back to normal."

"I looked around: there was no one within three feet of me. No one looked back, made eye contact, or stopped to claim responsibility. Fortunately, I was early for my flight. I ducked into the lounge of an empty gate, took out my journal – fumbled for and then kept dropping my pen because my hand was shaking so much - finally filling a page with as many variations of 'thank you' I could think of: 'gracias, danke, merci, gracie, spasiba' – block letters, script, large and small. I almost missed my flight."

"Wild, uh," she said, shaking her head. "What a day that was."

"Well, there continue to be reminders — especially when I doubt myself - always some chance occurrence reconnecting me to my Soul, my core — reminding me that I am not alone."

"The other day, for example, I was sketching some flowers and felt beckoned to look at one of them closely. Looking into the center of the flower, I could see and feel it pulsating. Although there was not even a hint of a breeze, the main petals as well as the pistil and stamen began to move, sway, then throb. I was awestruck."

"Every one of my mystical experiences has had that kind of impact — as if I was breaking through some invisible veil — revealing time and again that my — our - everyday world is filled with and surrounded by some greater reality."

"Looking into the center of the flower, I could see and feel it pulsating. Although there was not even a hint of a breeze, the main petals as well as the pistil and stamen began to move, sway, then throb. I was awestruck."

Sally then stopped, and took a few deep breaths. She felt one and then another hand on her arm.

"I don't care what any one says," she said softly, tears streaming down her face. "My insights and intuitions are true, genuine, because they are *real* experiences – not just some thought about an alleged God, or the recitation of a creed, or participation in a religious ritual which may help others but no longer holds any relevance for me."

"And my experiences are not *extra*-sensory or beyond my ordinary senses - because they involve my everyday senses. They are direct sensory encounters with what I can only call, 'the spiritual realm'. They don't make me better than anyone else or excuse me from dealing with my challenges. But they help to sustain me. They're alive and tangible and affirming. And they certainly confirm the existence of a spiritual reality that is both very understanding and very loving."

And Then There Were Four

"Oh, there is one other thing. I promise to stop after that," said Sally laughing to herself, "but as you know it is important to realize there are millions of people who have had similar experiences but dismiss them as silly - caused by a bad stomach, the result of overly extended emotions, or some such thing. Or worst, some do share with family or friends but then are so ridiculed that they learn to keep their secrets to themselves."

"Well," said Sally, "there is at least one other who has learned to affirm his spiritual experience. Initially he looked at me as if I was crazy – when I told him about the flower and the voice in the airport. But soon thereafter, he had an experience of his own. Did he ever apologize! Then he too became open to the possibility that the spiritual realm was not just a reference in the holy books - but could actually be a real, live encounter."

"His name is Brian. He is a poet and musician. He is my best friend - and now *my boyfriend.* We are to meet tonight — at 6:30. Want at least to say hello? I am sure he would enjoy knowing there were two other woo-woos on the planet."

No Tray, No Nothing

Brian was as tall and lanky as Sally was short and petite. He also had curly red hair, and wore the biggest, happiest smile you ever saw. The words that flowed from his mouth literally had an Irish lilt to them — the influence of his grandparents — who were originally from 'the old country', as Brian called it, and with whom he lived since the age of three following the death of his parents in a car accident.

"What? You want me to go blabbering about 'my encounter'", he said, holding up fingers for quotation marks. "So you say they are kin-folk – but they look mighty suspicious to me," he said laughing, swishing and twisting his face at Sam and Rhonda.

"Bri-an. Be nice!" said Sally.

"Okay, okay – let me at least order a beer, and then I'll go public before God - and everyone else who will listen."

"He's impossible, but I love him nonetheless."

The waiter arrived with three bottles and four glasses.

"I'll just have a sip of his," smiled Rhonda. Sam rolled his eyes.

Sally reviewed the main outlines of what transpired that afternoon, how excited and relieved the three of them were to find each other, and how she then invited Rhonda and Sam to come along and meet "my beau" – because, as Sally put it, "you, my dear, have both credentials and a potential role in all this as well."

"Meaning, I presume, my train story?"

"*The* train story - yes Brian dear, and any of the other things you care to share."

"Ooo-kay," he began. "It was about a year ago. My grandfather was ill and we needed money. And I was frazzled, working two and sometimes three jobs, exhausted most of the time, not eating much to save money. Crazy, stupid but at the time I decided that's what the situation demanded."

"So one night, late, I fell asleep on the train and rather than getting off at my stop, slept through it all and literally woke up in the train yard, alone. The car was empty, everyone else had obviously gotten off, and it's 'who in gawd's name' knows what time it is?"

"I checked my cell phone and the battery was dead; I realized that it had been getting weaker and weaker for days but had done nothing about it. I checked both cars – the one in front and the one in back of mine. Nothing. I was scared and started to yell out. Nothing. Then the door between one of the cars opened and in walked a small child carrying a tray of food - I swear to God, a small child carrying a tray of food. I well near lost it – I was so stunned."

"All she said was, 'Hi. Don't worry. You will be fine. Eat some food. It will nourish your body - and your spirit.'"

"I looked down at the tray of food. When I looked back up – the young girl was leaving. I called out. The door closed. Nothing. Then her earlier words registered like a loving command, and since I was indeed hungry – I ate, what I don't recall, but I ate all of it – including, this I do remember - including a piece of apple pie for dessert – my favorite."

"Then I fell asleep again – only to be awakened by a repairman who – as it turns out – had been sent out to search for me."

"Ben, Ben," he hollered, "he's here's just like the caller said. Seems fine. You best call the police just in case. He may need a ride home. Yeah: I'll bring him forward."

"What about the tray and stuff?" I asked the workman, suddenly acting like some variation on 'Mister Neatnik'.

"What tray?" he asked.

"I looked around. There was no tray in sight. No dishes, no shiny silverware, no nothing."

"Ooooo-kay, that's just grand," I thought to myself. "Best not ask any more questions – at least not yet."

"So I reached up - held the gentleman's arm - and he led me out – car, by car, by car. It was morning. The police were nice. They bought me home - right to me doorstep."

Spiritual Dimensions

"That's unbelievable," said Rhonda, lightly clapping her hands. "I love it. I have never heard anything like it."

"It's probably good you did not find the tray – or even a spoon. Some wildly religious group may have wanted to buy it and turn it into a shrine," added Sam.

"Based on my current finances, I might have sold it – and to the highest bidder."

"And the little girl – an angel, I presume?" Rhonda asked.

"Don't know. Were we closer to the Boston Garden, I might have thought she was queen of the leprechauns – up from beneath the floor-boards."

"Brian – don't kid."

"What else am I to think? An angel, yeah, an angel, I guess. What else could she have been? I can still see her – plain as day. And I can still taste that apple pie. Of all the things that were on that tray of food, that is the taste that still lingers – shades of an earlier apple tree, perhaps,

only this time this recipient definitely felt nourished versus shunned and excluded."

"And strangest thing of all, I did not eat for an entire four days thereafter – had no need to – was not hungry – never felt better. It must have been true manna from heaven."

"Sounds like the common theme of all our adventures," said Sam. "A new awareness followed by a sense of inclusion."

"And each – in a different way - breaks through the veil that ordinarily keeps us from experiencing 'the other side'," added Rhonda.

"Yet look how varied and unique our experiences have been," said Sally. "You – Brian - and the angelic girl; me and the trail of messages and the shimmering flower; and you, Rhonda – I didn't hear the whole story but apparently it involved a vision of a cosmic ball of light; and Sam, I overheard some reference to flying through space."

"Ball of light, and space travel?" asked Brian, his eyes wide, his brows up, his month open – all in mock amusement.

"Oh, sorry," said Rhonda. "Sally – you really have not been properly introduced to Sam's adventure, or the specifics of my vision. And Brian – you know nothing about either of our stories … yet. If you want, we can fill the both of you in now… at least give you the broad outlines. We'll save all the fascinating details for another time."

"Ohhhh – myyy," said Brian. "I guess it would be impolite if I now tried… to slowly… tip-toe out the door?"

Sharing and Critiquing

"Now, before we go much further, let's double-check. Are we crazy? Exaggerating? Wanting to believe something so badly that we let our imaginations run away with us?" asked Rhonda.

"Well, as Sam and I now each summarize, and I mean 'summarize' our experiences," Rhonda continued, "I think it would help the process, if, at the end, the other three play the role of devil's advocate. This way, we can test each other a bit – and make sure we are not getting carried away with our own enthusiasm."

"We owe ourselves to do at least that," said Brian with his usual jovial slant on everything. "If I did not have to defend the veracity of my story to the likes of the three of you, I might go and forget the bloody thing – then cease to believe that some low-brow like me could really have such an extraordinary experience."

"Besides," he added, "I want to feel prepped if ever interviewed by a leading magazine or Hollywood wants to buy the rights."

"Don't worry, Brian," said Molly in one of her rare repartees, "your low brow status will always be safe with us."

So all four decided: henceforth anyone's extra-ordinary story, dream, intuition or experience would be subject to the questions posed by the others. Rhonda quickly volunteered to go first. Sam went next. Molly then agreed to face the group's questions as she told her story again.

Brian had a slightly different take on things. "Hey," he said with a quivering voice, "it is getting a mite late and, as you know, I just told my story. Can't I await 'til next time to face interrogation by da mob – say in some really darkened room – bravely wincing under the glare of a bare million-watt light bulb."

"Now, Brian, now!" was the unanimous response.

The sessions went well. They each answered all questions put to them – except those no one could really explain - like why spirit appeared to them in the particular ways it did. None of them, however, changed their story, or the conviction that they had indeed experienced something from what they now referred to as 'the Spiritual realm'.

Inviting Others

"Of course we won't become an organization of any sort – not like the Rotary, a political party, or a religion," said Rhonda laughing, "but in affirming ourselves as having what can only be described as a 'spiritual experience', won't it be nice to invite others to affirm themselves as well. I am thinking of the hundreds if not thousands of people who are alone, thinking maybe they are crazy, too shy or battle-worn to go public - yet still wanting to affirm what was a very significant and intensive experience."

"At the same time," said Sam, "people all over the globe are confessing publicly to their belief in Spirit – as propagated by the various religions. Such stories are sacred to the believers but which - by ordinary standards – are also preposterous. But they have become so familiar that they are now treated as sacrosanct: the parting of seas, the burning bush, the incarnation of God, a virgin mother, the presence of God in a wafer, miracles galore, the devil, the reality of a heaven and a hell – on and on."

"So be it," said Sally, "and more power to those who hold such beliefs. Yet most of those foundational stories are admittedly irrational and are accepted only on trust or faith. Most important, they are not based on the believer's personal experience but either happened to or were recorded by people living thousands of years ago."

"So what's so different with our testimonies?" asked Rhonda. "Aren't they miraculous by any standard? The problem for society is that they have been experienced - not by formally holy or religious people – but by the unaffiliated - who just happen to believe wholeheartedly in their spiritual experiences and identity."

"We are not trying to contradict, question or undermine belief in the historical stories of formalized religion," murmured Brian. "And our experiences do not deal with anything but the miraculous presence of God and the loving and caring nature of the Spiritual Universe. Why

then would our stories be so threatening and our experiences labeled as silly or crazy?"

Suddenly, everyone was talking at once.

"I'll tell you why," said one. "Because we are audacious enough to say we have had what can only be described an 'other worldly' or sacred experience. But our experiences did not happen under the auspices, or with the approval of, an established religion."

"Yeah - the religious groups repeat their stories about revered historical figures, but we – unaffiliated and the ordinary people - who've had a direct experience of the spiritual, are in essence, treated like chopped liver."

"So we live and let live - wish the religions and their devotees well and also get on with our own lives. In fact, I still practice and admire some aspects of the religion bequeathed to me at birth. Obviously, based on the negative feedback that awaits anyone who says they have experienced some aspect of 'Spirit' directly, we know enough not to shout about it from the hilltops. Yet let's hope that never stops us from affirming what we have experienced."

"And thank God we live in such relatively tolerant times. Folks used to be burned at the stake for admitting what we have."

"So what is there - really - to stop us from encouraging others to share their experiences as well."

"Okay. I got it. Why not adopt the phrase we used earlier and declare ourselves to be *Kindred Spirits?* – which is what we are – and then let others know we would love to hear from them as well."

"Yes! We could open a website, summarize what has happened for us, and invite others to share – not their beliefs or hopes – but only what they consider their direct encounters with Spirit. No organization, no dues, no meetings, no conventions, no collections – just mutual honoring and respect."

"I love it."

"Me too."

"Sounds great."

"Well," said the last of the four, with mock impatience, "please realize, of course, that some of us may have already experienced our quota of miracles for a lifetime, so we may not have much to add or update on any regular basis."

"Nevertheless," he continued, deftly retreating toward the door, "if all this gets us to see each other more often, … *and* … if we have the opportunity to share our stories over a beer or two, then I guess it would be all right with me too."

"In that case," said Brian as he walked slowly toward the door, "and in that case only," he concluded with a dramatic wave of his right hand, "you may assume you can count on my periodic but *very firm* support." He then quickly opened and scampered out the door, leaving behind a hail of popcorn and paper cups.

The Experiences Deepen and Vary

So it was that Sam, Rhonda, Sally and Brian each continued to have an occasional experience of 'spirit' – some dramatic and others merely suggestive brushes with 'the other side'. As promised, each encounter was then 'tested' by the resident group of devil's advocates, a process that tended to eliminate anything less than a genuine experience. And such explorations not only strengthened the spiritual identity of the individual storyteller. It also served to intensify the group's sense of trust and camaraderie.

Sam, for example, on several occasions, experienced the person walking toward him, or standing next to him in an elevator – to be his duplicate or some slight variation on himself. He would also occasionally feel a sudden surge of energy in and around his head – and soon

treated it as a sign that spiritual energy, in the form of information or insight, was being infused into his awareness.

What Sam learned to trust the most was the receipt of a jolt of energy that shook his head slightly - indicating his Guardian Angel or other spiritual presence was immediately present. The jolt - or lack of one - would also be felt when he asked for guidance, posed a question or asked for feedback on a proposed course of action.

Rhonda had a recurring dream of life moving across a huge chess-board – newborns on one end and aging-wisdom on the other – all to a soft voice overlay that repeated the line, "life is ceaseless and immortal." Affirming words and phrases also continued to appear here and there. 'Be light', for example, appearing on an envelope she just happened to pick up, and then reappeared two days later as an underline in a book she purchased at a used bookstore.

Books on spiritual themes she could not find easily at the bookstore would suddenly fall into her lap as she combed the aisles. One morning, she awoke to the silhouette of an orchestra framed against her bedroom wall and the sound of some of the loveliest music she had never heard.

Sally, on the other hand, would intermittently find herself literally lost in time as she went about her day. She could become mesmerized, for example, by the new buds on trees and the emerging leaves of flower stems – especially when viewed through a magnifying lens. The same thing happened when she recorded birds and the gurgling sound of streams, or admired, interacted with and then took pictures of animals, babies and elderly people.

Most wondrous of all, she painted a series of large canvasses that looked to her colleagues like variations on what 'heaven' might look like: overlays of lush and loving swirls - light blue and rose with tints of gold and purple. She had sold two of them already – which greatly alleviated her budget problems – and had just received two commissions, one from a church and the other from a marketing firm.

As for Brian, his outer humor and sociable nature began to be balanced with more introspection — and then a regular diet of prayer and meditation. Then he discovered that his hands began to vibrate whenever he was near someone who appeared to be ill or badly out of sorts.

"So I began to gently raise or point my hands in someone's direction as I passed them: no fan fare, just innocently intending love with my hands," he told his colleagues. "Energy is energy. I thought maybe it would help. Then I saw a sign at a local church advertising a workshop on 'Use Your Healing Ways.' I went, felt at home, loved the people, so volunteered to work with whoever thought I/we could help. And a lot of people have been coming by."

"What exactly do you do?" asked Rhonda.

"Well, I realized we are all potential conduits for healing," he said calmly. "My hands are especially receptive. So I just hold them open and convey what God sends through me to anyone who wishes to receive it. God is the Source. I or we, as so-called healing agents, only help to convey or complete God's communication."

The Group Dynamics

As to the foursome, they, of course, met frequently as friends but only formally once a month - when any spiritual issue was explored or new testimony discussed. When there was no formal agenda, they simply communed, prayed and meditated together.

As to the group dynamics, the process of sharing was a genuinely new experience; none of them had ever listened - or been listened to - so intensely and thoroughly before. Each meeting thus had such an uplifting effect that they likened them to general 'energy boosts'.

Included in the ritual of each gathering was the raising of one's beer, wine or fruit juice for the customary parting toast - their

meetings being strategically located at the back room of McSorley's Bar and Grill.

And the cycle was never complete without a parting word or gesture from the group's resident court jester. He had mellowed but not that much. The group called it, 'Brian's Inevitable Rant and Rave.' So it was that on this particular occasion Brian stood, raised himself to his full height of six feet, three inches – and in full Irish-American swagger, rapped on the top of the table.

"Ah, may I have your attention please," he began.

"I sense it is the time – finally," he said with great gusto, "this being our anniversary or twelfth such monthly meeting, a milestone to be sure" – and he was immediately interrupted with applause from his colleagues.

"And, thus," he continued, waving both open arms, "this is indeed the best and most appropriate time - as they used to say in the old Irish neighborhoods of the Bronx - to seal the deal, if you will, by... by.... yes, folks, you know what it is... by... not only developing a club handshake, not only devising a team song, ta-tah, but..."

"But, wait, there is more," he said in typical sales lingo, "this is also the time for each of us to buy tee-shirts with the common logo of 'Kindred Spirits' emblazoned front ... and rear!"

"And I," he concluded, "as the resident entrepreneur, am here to take your orders.... Sizes please!"

This time, however, Brian apparently miscalculated and spoke a bit too soon. He was still in the middle of the room with his chair between him and the doorway.

With no easy or visible means of escape, he was dutifully and directly pelted - mid-sentence, mind you - with a barrage of flying pretzels and cheese puffs. And true to his beliefs and stature - and having badly out-foxed himself - he stood and took it... head tilted back, mouth wide

open. Fairing none too well, he finally stooped to retrieve and return a few remnants of his own.

Wait Until You Hear About This

"Hey, Sam, where've you been. I've been trying to reach you all weekend," said Scott, his camera in one hand and notebook in the other.

"Does your early appearance on a Monday morning mean you have already taken the photos for our lead stories?" asked Sam.

"Not exactly," said Scott, "what I want to talk about has more to do with what is in my notebook than my camera."

"You suddenly a writer – the essence of the Renaissance man?"

"No, no – something totally different. You know how we kid you all the time about your 'spooky' stuff – well, not today. Today I come to you with a spooky story of my own. I am not kidding or putting you on. This is serious and I don't know who else to turn to."

"Okay, Scott. You've got my attention."

"You know that my Mom's been sick, really sick. The docs think it is the Big C. You and others are always telling me to keep a journal – as if I did not write enough notes on each picture. But – I know – a journal is not reporting on things or people; it is reporting on yourself: your own emotions and feelings, especially as they relate to what's going on is your life. That much I know."

"So last Thursday," he continued, "I sit down to write some things on my computer after returning from the hospital. I begin with the operation, and my sadness – and before I realized it I was writing this very long letter to God – about how much I wanted my Mother to survive and asking God to make that possible. Three, no four hours later – I look up to discover it is past midnight. And the stuff I have written – about God and the power of prayer and my need to open my

mind and my heart - reads like something out of some ancient text: the language is almost biblical in nature."

"As you know I can rattle off the sentences as well as anyone when I have to but have a hard time understanding, or quoting, Dickens – no less a prophet of old. Where did this stuff come from? Did I have my brain rewired? Is somebody following me around and putting recordings into my Bluetooth? And – to think - I filled 26 pages with this stuff. It took hours. I remember only sitting down – and then later, getting up. I at least had the sense to print it out in a hard copy. Maybe it's encouraging me to slow down, study it, interpret its messages, take its words to heart … and see if and how it relates to me and my Mother."

"Dumbfounded - does not begin to describe my confusion," he continued. "And I both want to delve into it and yet am hesitant to do so. It is all so strange. Frankly - now please don't hassle me – it feels like the voice of my grandfather who was religious, I mean, really religious. Is it him – or some part of me – who's telling me things I need to hear? I'm scared and frankly, I'm humbled. Have I neglected something important for too long? Am I a woo-woo after all?"

"If you are, I am sure you are destined to be a wonderful one," said Sam laughing. "Now first, please sit, relax. Just close your eyes for a minute and just breath."

The Gift of Automatic Writing

Ten – fifteen – seconds go by.

"Okay, I am still breathing," says Scott.

"I can see that," Sam responded, laughing himself. "And your eyes are still closed. You are a veritable yogi. Please continue to just breathe deeply with your eyes closed – just a little bit longer."

"In the meantime, please don't be in such a hurry to figure everything out. You have been gifted with a message – one that came

through you as 'automatic writing'," Sam said in a soft and almost fatherly tone. "Where does it come from? Some say God, or an angel, or - from what you say about the ancient sounding style of the language - it could be the Soul of an ancient spiritual writer or mystic. Others also attribute the messages they receive via automatic writing to the release of insights long known by some deeper part of themselves, aspects of the Soul they had never before been open enough to acknowledge."

"Either way, twenty-six pages is nothing to ignore. Trust it. It came through you – why? That's what you are about to discover. Go with it. Learn from it. Some spiritual aspect outside or inside of you beckons to you. Either way - consider it a wondrous gift – an invitation to learn more about yourself, your Mother, your relationship, and the spiritual universe in which we live. Continue to be open - to recall more details. Write them down too. And be aware of the possibility of more automatic writing being gifted to you in the future. You might even be inclined to expand upon what you've already written – a sort of chapter two or three. If so, then go with it."

Scott opened his eyes.

Sam pulled up a chair.

"Mind if I say one more thing?" Sam asked.

"Please: I am still dazed - but what you say is very helpful."

"How many people do you know, Scott, who have been so blessed as to receive the honor of automatic writing? I congratulate you. I always told you: you are much more than the pictures you take of others. This time your lens is pointing at and into yourself. So it feels strange. It should. It's new. But, believe me, it is a gift and I urge you to treat it that way."

"Haw, okay. I like that," Scott responded, his hand stroking his chin. "I will read it all carefully. Maybe, I'll even do some more! Either way, I'll get back with you. Thanks. Sam. I really appreciate it."

"Any time."

As they paused to go, Sam tugged gently on Scott's sleeve. "Now, please, don't forget about the pictures you also need to take for the paper," he said with a big smile.

"No problem," said Scott. "No problem, I assure you. Adding to my repertoire by also learning how to point my lens inward – does not mean I have forgotten how to focus on the traditional stuff."

Time Goes By

Weeks, months, then several months went by.

The group of four continued to meet regularly – with the exception of responding to one 'emergency' request from Sally, and three weeks later, a nonchalant e-mail from Brian that read, "please – can I buy everyone a beer. Soon, please: I am really thirsty." The issues raised by each party were resolved and/or clarified. Both involved a mixture of spirituality and romance, as you might expect.

As to the fate of "Kindred Spirits", the foursome did develop a website - complete with text, photos of nature scenes and original art pieces. The headings included "Listening to Your Inner Spirit," "Come Out of the Spiritual Closet", "Honor Your Extra-Ordinary Experiences" and "Connecting with Other Kindred Souls."

The site attracted a lot of attention. And as the weeks and months went by the comments and the stories grew in volume. It was then that they realized how widespread the spiritual experience was - and how varied it could be. People reported having glimpses of - or interventions from - 'the other dimensions' through dreams, intuitions, chance meetings, so-called coincidences, sudden insights, answers and resolutions of issues received during or shortly after meditation, and direct encounters with either a 'very spiritual person' or what were often described as 'a field of energy' or 'presence'.

And such experiences involved every aspect of the senses: for some the message or contact came through hearing, while sight and touch were dominant for others. Some were involved directly in an event — like Brian and the girl with the food — while others sensed something 'very real' but which they could not hear or see.

The combined experiences certainly served to solidify the group's conviction that some aspect of everyone's common humanity enabled them to have all sorts of direct contacts with the 'spiritual realm' — that is, once a person overcame their fears or false humility. For want of a clearer description, the website soon referred to the "innate capacity of every Soul to experience and interact directly with Spirit."

Of course, loonies from the overly zealous religious right and the 'oh so sophisticated naysayers on the left initially called that common empowerment either 'heresy' or 'hallucinatory'. But finding no one to fight or even argue with, both sets eventually took their smarty-pants venom elsewhere.

Otherwise, the reception was lovely and loving. Lots of folks submitted lots of amazing stories — leading to many reviews, the making of many new friends, and finally a book of entries that celebrated each experience as well as the spirit of mutual honoring.

An Unusual Request

It was sometime during the following winter that Sam received an unusual request. Roy, still the paper's most adventurous, no nonsense and skeptical reporter, asked Sam if he could cover a story that was causing a buzz in the local restaurants, athletic clubs and chat rooms.

"Something about a set of people interested in 'spiritual themes'," said Roy, using his fingers as quote marks. "Nothing religious — or so they say — just a group that allegedly honors everyone's so-called 'innate spirituality' and capacity to receive angelic guidance."

He hesitated, then continued: "But if their theme has any merit - sans clergy, creeds and collections – of course it could be a blessing. I'm skeptical but I would like to investigate," he said.

He began to walk away, looked back and added: "I may even have 'a spiritual experience' to share with the group myself. What say you? A few columns for next week's edition."

"Hey, Roy: go for it. But be sure to include your own testimony. In fact, I think that is a must. Make it sort of a first-person commentary, combining your usual third-party reporting with your newly acquired personal experience."

"Haw," said Roy. "A sort of analytic true confessions, huh? Okay. I'll give it a try. Who knows what might be revealed?"

A long silence - then Roy's voice shouting from down the hall: "Maybe the group has some single woman in it, someone special who would love to share a beer – with, say, an aspiring journalist – some guy who has dreamed - of traveling – say, in space – out-of-body."

"Could be, Roy. Miracles do happen," said Sam - laughing - as he speed dialed Rhonda on his i-phone.

Choices

The Wondrous Ways of Reincarnation

A delightful set of characters find themselves

walking through a long tunnel into a well lit stadium —

only to discover that they have departed their Earthly life

and have returned to the realm of Pure Spirit.

Their off-hand selections of 'heaven' or 'hell'

are soon replaced by in-depth reviews

of everything they chose to create and why

during their recent incarnation on Earth.

Not punished but greatly enlightened,

each one chooses to re-incarnate on Earth

with the intent of creating greater love and joy.

Dazed

I felt a jot. It did not hurt but it did feel strange, different. It registered as a deep but cushioned 'zong'. I felt it first in the middle of my chest. Then it resounded throughout my body. I tried but could not open my eyes yet was aware only of a haze which grew increasingly thick and dark.

Had someone lifted a window and let in bursts of fog, or turned on a smoke machine from some nightclub? Even the outlines of faces faded gradually as I was encouraged to relax by soft but invisible voices. The message was clear: 'Don't struggle. All is well. Simply allow myself to fall into a heavy and reassuring sleep.'

The blare of flickering lights surprised me - as did the sound of furniture being moved, a cold hand on my wrist, and then a face – up close then fading away. As I phased in and out of consciousness, all I could remember was the sight of a cheekbone, the side of a nose and a large eye socket with long eyelashes.

The bursts of pressure on my chest startled me. But again I faded in and out of consciousness – remembering only a cadence of numbers, fingers tugging at my tongue, and the scent of peppermint as warm lips blew puffs of air into my mouth.

I tried to speak but my body was numb. I just wanted to tell both the soft and the loud voices that I was fine and to let me be. I just wanted to sleep. Besides, wasn't it obvious I was choosing to transit back home to the realm of Spirit?

A few words – then only syllables - each successive grunt more gobbled, laborious and elongated than the one before, far away soundings – as if from the depths and recorded at slower and slower speeds. Gradually everything receded – and finally stopped.

It was then that I heard singing.

The Old Neighborhood

The pinhole of light became larger and brighter, eventually zooming into an over-sized doorway surrounded by alternating colored lights. As I stepped onto a moving stairway, I could hear voices and music – Gregorian chant followed by Dvorak's 'New World Symphony'. And then, zoom: I was propelled into a large well-lit open-air stadium. I felt

like an Olympian runner suddenly emerging from a subterranean tunnel into the fullness of daylight.

"Please, no applause," I snickered.

Then a welcoming voice: "Ah, William. We thought you were about to be delayed," it said. "But finally all those nice people let you go. Welcome home. I'm Nathaniel, your Guardian Angel. Please come on through the gate into this area here near the fountain."

"Okay," I said, feeling both hesitant and reassured. I also quickly realized I was in no position to argue.

"As I stepped onto a moving stairway, I could hear voices and music — Gregorian chant followed by Dvorak's 'New World Symphony'."

Revisiting

I bowed my head instinctively to the figure before me. I did not recognize him - yet he seemed strangely familiar. I knew *I knew* him,

but from where? He looked thoroughly human: blue jeans and a tee shirt, tall - perhaps six foot three — and although his face had a classic mature wisdom to it, his demeanor and energy were very youthful, and — unlike me - had a full head of hair. He was human all right, or at least looked like one of us. Then I realized there was one very major difference: the edges of his body were surrounded by shimmering light.

"Welcome home," Nathaniel said with a big smile. "You have made the transition back to your original birth place. As an immortal Soul, you may recall that you chose to incarnate or assume a bodily form on Earth, and thus transited from here to the physical realm — by your count - many years ago, but much, much less according to relative timelessness on this side."

He laughed. "Let me say that again - slowly: you are an immortal spirit... who just finished spending a few years having an Earthly experience. A few minutes ago you decided to surrender your mortal body on Earth ...and thus have returned ...to your eternal birth place ... here in the realm of Pure Spirit."

He waited. I gulped, then frowned, pursed my lips — and breathing deeply —tried to make a conscious effort to understand.

"In essence, you have been going to school," said the angelic being, "going to the school of applied knocks, so to speak, learning how to implement the principles of love and compassion — in concrete and specific ways - in the material universe."

Still stunned, I just listened.

"Earth is not always an easy experience," he said. "Although you had some joyous and delightful experiences, we know you've also been through many difficulties and faced many challenges. Most important, you learned a lot and progressed a great deal, doing many of the things you said you would complete when you left here — last time and reincarnated again on Earth."

Nathaniel then motioned to a number of figures that were waiting on the side of the gate to greet and welcome me back. "Oh my", I heard my mother cry. And beside her - my father, both sets of grandparents, my brother, and some of my teachers and friends from my old neighborhood – all of who had passed many years before. And there – as well – were beloved friends and mentors from various periods of the life I had just completed.

It was like old home week as we hugged, and chatted, and hugged some more - laughing and reminisced about the old days - which somehow still seemed to exist.

Finally, a slight tap on the shoulder: "William, it is time to make more sense of all this," said Nathaniel. "The transition from Earth back home can be very confusing. So we want to re-introduce you to the facets of this eternal life. Then we will help you complete a review of your latest assignment – or as we call it 'your latest incarnation' - on Earth."

Introducing the Spiritual Realm

He then assured me that "we'll take it one step at a time - to make sure you feel perfectly comfortable and recall everything you want to – and, I might add, at a pace that feels right to you."

"O-kay," I said with a growing sense of confidence. Then I noticed my greeting party had disappeared - and apprehension returned. Where to now? I kept looking around me, like a tourist in Times Square – both curious and protective - as Nathaniel guided me to a set of cushioned chairs next to a low-lying table. There, to my delight, was the spiritual equivalent of my morning favorites: hot coffee and a few slices of crusty French bread. As I reached for some sugar and butter, Nathaniel opened a large folder and a colorful looking scrapbook.

"First, the preliminary overview. Then you can choose what you prefer to do next. Sound okay?" he asked.

"Yes, of course," I replied, still unsure but feeling increasingly more confident and comfortable. Wherever I was, I sensed, I had been here many times before - here in this place now also being referred to as 'home central'. In fact, as I looked around, I recognized other familiar faces and some very familiar surroundings. Besides, nobody was lunging at my chest any longer, although I wondered what had happened to *that* woman and her peppermint breath. But now, rather than wanting to fall asleep, I very much wanted to be alert and fully present.

"As we have noted already, and you are slowly coming to realize: you have just completed a major transition – this one from your most recent incarnation as an embodied being on Earth. Thus you have returned to your spiritual home where you can reclaim the fullness of your prime reality as an immortal Soul."

I took a deep breath, nodded slowly, and finally said, "This still feels a bit strange, but it is also beginning to feel right. I am still partially dazed, but all this – you, the transit, the surrounding - are beginning to make sense … a least I think they are beginning to make sense."

"No hurry," said my radiant friend with a big smile. "Let's assume we have all the time in the world, which we do – literally – since immortality is timeless. So please relax and experience the emotional solace of your coffee and bread. Of course, you no longer need to consume anything here in order to sustain your existence and wellbeing. As a pure spirit, all that is now on automatic."

He then suggested I finish my coffee, relax, observe the surroundings and absorb the impact of what I'd just gone through. He had received a call from someone on Earth who apparently needed his help immediately. He assured me he would return promptly.

"No problem," I uttered, "I'll be right here. I'm fascinated with the steady stream of the people – I mean, Souls! - who keep emerging from the tunnel. For some reason, I am particularly interested in this next set - now coming through the gate."

Assignments: One to the Left

"Hey," said a husky guy — in his early sixties - by the name of Danny. "Is this hell?"

"Why? Are you expecting hell?" asked the iridescent figure at the gate - a colleague of Nathaniel.

"Yeah: all my life I was told I was a sinner — so what else should I expect?"

"It all depends on the kind of life you think you led while on Earth?"

"Well, I laughed a lot, danced a lot, raised a ruckus here and there, carried a rifle in two wars, and got mighty flirtatious if I had one too many. It drove my wife crazy - which might explain why I was married three times. On the really good side, however, I have three kids — great kids every one of them."

"Are you sure that merits going to hell?"

"I don't think I've exactly earned a berth in heaven," he said with a hardy laugh. "And by the way, what do you mean 'while on Earth'? Where exactly am I now?"

"You can't remember transiting, eh?" asked the guide. "Well, first, there are some folks over there - the ones waving to you — who would like to say hello. Take your time, visit for a while - just relax. Someone will soon come to fetch you, and then we'll commence the formal tour — and make arrangements for your placement."

The cry of "Danny, you little sweetheart you" — was followed by the oncoming crush of what sounded like a dozen family members and friends. Based on the greetings, it was obvious Danny was loved - but not universally; a few others hung back, scowls on their faces. Still, on balance, it seems like a joyous homecoming. Danny certainly seemed to be enjoying it.

As soon as the backslapping and the storytelling began to wind down, a tough looking angel wearing a torn shirt and baseball cap suddenly appeared. He called Danny over, then came right to the point: "You wanted hell, you get hell. Okay! Just take this road of hot coals to the left. Understand? Go about a ten miles, more or less. Ignore the faucets. They have never worked. They're there just to tease and bug you. After a while you'll see the signs - and believe me – you'll feel the heat and hear the screams."

"Anybody else going my way?" asked Danny.

"Are you kidding?", said the Angel with a broad smile. "We haven't recovered yet from the overload caused by Dante's Inferno. Just follow that long line winding over the hill and around that mountain."

Danny shuffled on, and up stepped the next person to the gate, a small and elderly lady, maybe in her early eighties, wearing a box hat and veil, and tightly gripping her large black purse.

Assignments: This One to the Right

"Heaven, can you direct me to heaven, please," she asked.

"So you think heaven exists, and that heaven is the place for you?"

"Young man, I assure you I have kept the Lord's Day each week for 82 years. I always volunteered to run bingo and serve at the bake sales. Recently, I even cared for an elderly person and two sick cats. Where else do you think I belong?"

"If that is what you have in mind, then that is what you shall have. Initial placement here is based on one's belief systems and expectations."

"But that is only half of it," he lamented, winking to a colleague who had come to supervise the next shift at the turnstile. "The other half focuses on an assessment of your experience. Let's see. Regular

church attendance: 10 points. I'll give you another five for caring for the old lady and her cats. The bingo and bake sales really are not worth more than another three – giving you a total of 18 points, short of the mandatory 20. Got anything else?"

"Prayer, lots of prayers, and once I meditated," said the woman, soothing one hand with the other.

"Oh, prayers? Why didn't you say so? They are worth the most. Besides choosing heaven, it seems like you have also earned a reserved spot in the heaven of your choice."

Reaching in his pocket, he gave her a ticket that depicted an array of flowers circling the words, 'Paradise.'

"Now - all you need to do is walk a few steps down the boulevard to the right," said the Angel, "there that large one with the billboard reading *'Redemption'*. A cab driver, dressed in a long robe, and driving a light blue cloud, will whisk you up to the mountaintop."

The guide assured Miss Wanda Granderson that she would be comfortable and among a variety of people who consider themselves to be close to God: some will be clutching rosaries, he told her, while others will undoubtedly be preaching (to themselves or whoever will listen).

"There will also be a fair number of penitents flipping through their well-thumped Bibles," said the Angel, "and lots of folks talking in tongues. Their favorite word is 'hallelujah'. You'll also discover some who just love to sing and are always looking to enlist the new people in their choir."

"Oh," he quickly added, "a group of very nice counselors will soon help you to review all the particulars of your last incarnation on Earth. Until then, however, you have plenty of time to just wander around, see who you relate to the most, and enjoy yourself. If we don't hear from you, we'll assume you're happy. If not, just ring the bell. We work 24-7," he said with a knowing giggle.

Endings and Beginnings

And so it was that every one who had recently left their bodily remains on Earth was now well into the second and third phrases of their transit: having arrived safely, they were all welcomed to the non-denominational 'great beyond' by their deceased family and friends, and then given an initial placement that coincided with their beliefs and self-estimates.

It was enough of a shock for most to accept the fact that they'd left their bodily form behind, that those features and contours they buffed and polished so long and patiently were now history. So it took a while for any of them to fully accept the reality that their 'lifetime' on Earth, as they had known it – with all its interactions and issues, its many joys and worries and dreams – had come to an end.

At least there was no sense in asking for the location of the restrooms: that periodic urge was also a thing of the past. But then, who were these simmering beings who greeted us and now guide us? What and where was this new place with all its strangers – people, Souls, *whatever* - whose initial choices suggested we had something in common? Hmmmmm.

Besides, what happens now?

More Questions Than Answers

The faces of the other new arrivals seemed to exhibit the same concerns. "I was a person with a body, and a family, and a job - and at least some social life," one of them remarked, scratching his head. "Now I am simply referred to as 'Soul Samuel'. I am not sure which name is a reminder and which is prophetic. And look: I can put the outline of my so-called 'intentional hand' right through the outline of this ball of energy where my body used to be."

"Now that's worth writing home about!" said another. "But where would I send the letter, and what is my return address?"

A pamphlet distributed at the gate suggested the transitional process was by no means over. Although beliefs were being converted into self-fulfilling prophecies and self-assessments determined one's initial assignment, each Soul was also told they would be able to change their placement – or be asked to do - once they completed their reviews and evaluations.

The pamphlet was emphatic: "It should now be very clear that you have relinquished your bodily existence on a material Earth and transited to the realm of Pure Spirit. This is your true home, the realm into which you were created by God as an immortal Soul, from which you launched your last stay or incarnation on earth."

"If you find your initial assignment to be misguided or incomplete," it pointed out, "please do not fret or worry. We will get it all straightened out and help you attain whatever adjustments are warranted. But first, we will - together - review your previous incarnation on Earth, at which time you will receive the appropriate counseling and clarify what you wish to do next."

The conclusion: "Not only could your initial placement change but so could your choices regarding what you now want and wish to learn next. Thinking down the road a bit, don't be surprised if you also begin to consider what kind of lifeline you'd prefer to lead in your *next* incarnation on Earth."

Instantly came a question from the rear of the group: "Did you say, *'Choose a lifeline for our next incarnation?'"* – meaning we are destined to shuffle on back to Earth after all?"

"Is this Bellevue?" asked another. "I'm now having a difficult time breathing. I never thought I would say it, but 'Mein Gott'- but what the hell is going on here?'"

Some reacted differently. They seemed ready to roll with whatever unfolded, reasoning that the opportunity for transformation was so rare that they considered themselves privileged to be in a new place, faced with a new adventure, maybe – "if they are telling us the truth – even given the chance to plan for and create a new life."

"Wow: and there I was," said Danny. "A divorced salesman living in a run-down flat in Brooklyn, and now I may be able to revolutionize my life – and maybe even learn how not to be so selfish. Now that would be something."

Others, however - wearing sweatshirts reading *Really Old Soul* - immediately recognized the process as the miracle of continuous rein-carnation. Several nodded when one young man recalled "having gone through all this – in this very spot - many times before." In fact, many quickly recognized the tunnel and the initial gathering area as soon as they arrived. You could tell from their expressions that they were thinking: "been here, done this, so what's to worry?"

But while the demeanor of most of these self-proclaimed returnees suggested they were facing their reentry with relative ease and opti-mism, you could also tell from the furrowed brows that a few were still very nervous; perhaps some of the poignant details of their previous visits were starting to come through, enough to make them leery of what the latest review might reveal – and foretell.

Look at Who's Returning Home!

You could get a good sense of a Soul's state of consciousness by who greets them at the gate. A Soul's last Momma and Poppa and selected family members and close friends, of course, are always there. But then the greeting parties vary greatly - from the demeanor of the family and friends, and the appearance or absence of colleagues and community leaders.

One throng of greeters, for example, might include a Saint Francis, Moses or Gandhi, while another could attract the likes of 'Louie the Grunt", "Crazy Maisy" and "Attila the Hun." Based on a given Soul's background, spiritual progress and earned associations, any Soul then in residence could also show up. The likes of Rumi, Madame Blavatsky, Meister Eckhart and Simone Weil, for example, often come by to meet a returning Soul like Dag Hammarskold, Mother Teresa and many others who although relatively unknown in the material world had quietly earned the respect of the great adepts.

The stature of the greeters thus did not necessarily correspond to a returning Soul's Earthly rank or title; such things were irrelevant in the spiritual realm. Basic goodness - contributions to the community, and a record of embracing the norms of unconditional love — are what mattered the most. Thus a given Pope, TV evangelist, famous politician or movie star might only attract a few uncles and a wayward nephew, while the woman who ran the community center in an out-or-the-way village might be greeted by Carl Jung, Marcus Aurelius, Mary Magdalene and the bagpipers of heaven's own marching band.

It was the returning Souls with spiritually exalted friends who knew immediately that they are returning back home — that is as soon as they saw the bright light at the end of the tunnel. "Here it is again," they had reason to exclaim. "How fortunate are we to be returning to the Reality once more - after another stint in the physical realm. We learned a lot and were glad to contribute our little something to the Earth's continuance. But we are also tired and in need of some R and R. Living on Earth can be a tough slog."

Such Souls also realized that once their initial review was completed, they would be able to return to the beloved Learning Lab — that vast interactive center that has always served as both their launching pad and their welcome mat.

"Ah, to be back here again", was their dominant sentiment, "supported and encouraged by the infinite wisdom of the spiritual realm.

It is there that we are inspired to learn, to research and to plan how we wish next to serve the Kosmos. It is the most wondrous part of being an immortal Soul – to live knowing full well that we are part and parcel of the Creating God Itself, a contributing cell in the universal organism we call God.'

One's number of past lives - or the achievements attained within each - did not, of course, guarantee one's placement this next time around. That depended on what you did or did not do in your latest incarnation. Thus the oldest or most elevated Souls as well as the youngest or least accomplished, had to undergo an evaluation of their most recent lifetime as soon as they returned to the Spirit realm. And that involved an assessment of accomplishments and contributions relative to the standards they set for themselves prior to their 'descent'.

Attaining only a mixed record during an incarnation on Earth - that is, achieving only some aspects of one's Learning Contract – was not uncommon. Earth was a wild and wooly place that specialized in challenge, complexity and the temptation to either be so worldly as to be egotistical, or so 'saintly' as to be of no earthly good.

And as always, all returning Souls - both adept and apprentice alike – each returned with at least a few insights into how to be more loving and attain a greater wholeness – despite the temptation to embrace what was most self-serving and inconsequential. Such insights were shared during the evaluations and were then stored in the Learning Lab, serving as interactive commentaries for all those who were about to reenter the physical universe and face similar circumstances.

No Nothing

As it turns out, I came out of my transitional fog faster than expected, and not only began to sense that I had been here many times before, but started to recall some of the processes involved in what was referred to as 'spirituality'. So when Nathaniel had to excuse himself – for his

emergency fly-by and intervention on Earth somewhere – I thought nothing of it.

"No problem," I said, and reminded him I enjoyed watching - and learning from - the interactions at the gate.

Looking up, I noticed a man in his seventies exit the tunnel and approach the gate. Three steps behind him was a well-proportioned woman of around the same age.

"Are you Peter?" they asked, almost in unison.

"No, my name is Luigi," answered the guardian.

"Where's Peter?"

"I don't know. Anyone seen Peter?" he asked.

Someone shrugged, baring his open hands.

"Seems nobody has seen him in ages," Luigi concluded. "Do you want to come in - or do you have other plans?"

"You call these pearly gates," snickered the couple. "We're seen better in San Francisco. Okay, okay. So Peter doesn't exist. Admit it. I told those silly people surrounding my bed that all their conjecture and fanfare was make-believe. And now we can see for ourselves," said Edgar.

"No Peter, no heaven, no God, no nothing", said his partner who wore a tee-shirt with the inscription: 'My Name is Maude. That's Enough.'

"We've been writing about the big hoax for years," she said, putting down the large brief bag she managed, somehow, to bring with her. "So now we have the opportunity to see for ourselves."

"We have to tell the others," said Edgar with great excitement, "especially your holier-than-thou family. Sir: do you have a cell phone? We need to make a call."

"I am sorry but we not have any telephones here," said Luigi.

"Then how do you communicate? Twitter? Text? Tin cans? What?"

"Do you really want to know?" asked Luigi, looking up at Edgar, wrinkling his nose. "It might be too soon. If you knew the answer to that question, it might literally upset you — causing you even more confusion than having to acknowledge the indisputable fact, for example, that you both died this morning in Wellington, Indiana - at 10:05 and 10:06 a.m., respectively. Yet here you are interacting with us as if nothing had ever happened."

Luigi waited — then added: "There is no pearly gate, I grant you, but the reality is you both surrendered your bodies this morning following a car crash - and now *you* are here - *talk-ing to us!*" he said with emphasis. "Get it?"

There was a long silence. Finally, Edgar looked over to Maude and murmured, "hmmmm." She raised her eyebrows, shook her head, looked down - and sighed.

"Well it does seem like we are still alive — at least in some sense. It is all so strange," said one - "and incomprehensible," said the other.

They exchanged glances with Luigi.

"Do you mind if we just sit for a minute?"

"Of course, not," said Luigi. "Please. Can we get you something to eat? Coffee maybe? Some Danish … a piece of fruit?"

They smiled, pulled their coats around them. "That would be nice, thank you," said Edgar. "That would be very nice indeed. I must say: there is something about this place I am beginning to like."

"But don't relax," Maude quickly added, nodding her head, staring directly at Luigi. She then shook her index finger vigorously. "Don't forget: I'm still keeping an eye on you."

The Key Issue Is Raised

Nathaniel reviewed the information in my folder: name, age, the inclusive dates of my most recent incarnation, location and set of interim addresses, immediate family, and the list of formal activities like the when's and wherefores of schooling, jobs, marriage, parenting and general interests – plus a profile of main characteristics, intentions, creativity, contributions and missed opportunities.

"The info all seems in order," I said, "although I might dispute some of the descriptions and conclusions. But I love the pictures. Wherever did you get them all? I thought I would remember most of my life very clearly, but I can only vaguely recall some of these people and experiences. Giving someone a seat on a crowded bus, confronting a man hurting a child, sending a healing message to a woman in a wheelchair? Did any of that really matter?"

"Unless," I continued, "you are highlighting anything – big or small – that helped somebody in some way, even if it involved someone I never met again."

"That's it," said Nathaniel. "Who did you help, how did you contribute to others. Love, empathy, compassion: everything else is secondary."

"What about my education, my professions of faith, my career advancements, my hopes and dreams?" I asked.

"Window dressing." he said shaking his head. "Whatever so-called achievement - anyone points to - please know it is insignificant in itself. But if you use it to do something that contributes to the common good, or intentionally use an opportunity to help others and increase your capacity to love, then any and everything becomes significant. We are most interested in loving intentions and loving outcomes."

"Bishop or barmaid, A grades or C, parent or single, rich man or poor – it does not matter," he emphasized. "How you used your life circumstances, whatever they were, to increase your sensitivity - your

inner level of consciousness - by deliberately choosing to express empathy and exercise compassion - that's the most significant indicator of your spirituality and psychological wholeness. That's it. That's everything."

I must have looked puzzled. So he tried again: "It is all so simple that it's confusing, eh? This love stuff is so easy to talk about but very difficult to accomplish – which is why Souls like you keep going back, choosing one more incarnation, one more opportunity, to learn how to love more fully and in as many situations as possible."

There was a long silence.

"Why don't we take a break and you can just wander about the grounds," Nathaniel finally said to me with a broad smile. "It will give you a chance to think about your last incarnation in terms of this love-thing. And it will give me a chance to see how some others are doing."

Self-Fulfilling Prophecies

I returned to the reading material. Apparently there was a universal principle that applied to everyone and everywhere. It was the principle of the self-fulfilling prophecy – which was equally true on Earth as it was now in the spiritual realm. We created our own reality by attracting to us the circumstances needed to demonstrate and fulfill our images and expectations.

From one incarnation to the next, and certainly within each lifetime – one pamphlet emphasized - we always had the power to choose: circumstances, relationships, skills and abilities whatever came our way. Thus opportunities to act according to what we imaged and wished for would naturally appear - as would the consequences of our choices. Love in, love out. Garbage in, garbage out. Affirmations in, confirmations out. We literally had the capacity to set and fulfill our best dreams and our worst motivations.

The devil and my dastardly boss did not do it. I did. Likewise, the love I created – in the face of the challenges to do otherwise - was the direct result of my choices. We create what we conceive, contribute what we image – maybe not immediately or in exactly the same way we desired. But everything we intend and do - inevitably returns to us like a cosmic boomerang.

I played all this back to Nathaniel upon his return. He nodded and smiled. "I think you've got it," he said. "The reason Souls choose to return to Earth so often - in a new bodily form and under new circumstances - is because love and compassion, the major biggies, are always seeking greater and fuller expression."

"Incarnating in the material realm is your proving ground," he said, "giving you still one more opportunity to choose love - and express it as unconditionally and in as many ways as possible."

The Full Range of Experiences

As Nathaniel and I walked about the grounds and glided among the clouds, we could see and hear evidence of the principle of self-fulfilling prophecies. The most recent transients, for example, were living out a wide range of expectations. Some sang praises to the Lord while others moaned about the red devils and burning coals.

Still others, at least initially, were on their knees, some nodded repeatedly before an ancient wall, and some others seemed frozen in a sitting position. The selections filled the gambit, from Souls tearing their now imaginary clothes to folks parading in their Easter finery.

Among those presuming themselves saved were lots of Souls who had just returned from embodiments in many of the leading sects of the world's established religions. Upon review of their own assessments, their numbers seemed split three ways: those who were sure the blue and pink clouds indicated they were in the right place, those who were willing to accept an interim placement in 'purgatory' (as long as they

knew that would eventually elevate on up to heaven - without too much delay, that is), and the remaining third who clung to replica steeples, lecterns and hymnals as if fearful of eventual banishment.

Many who had thought the whole spiritual thing a hoax now tended to sit and hold their heads in their hands — or at least cradled it on one arm and an elbow. Lots of words reverberated within those alcoves, and lots of sighs too. "It doesn't compute," "such silliness", "this simply cannot be supported by science", "its all emotional nonsense", and "let's face it: we predicted a vacuum, we got a vacuum" - were the phrases invoked most often.

Among those who happily waved to us as we toured the premises were colorful celebrants of Shiva and Vishnu, and the many others bearing begging bowls and wearing pendants depicting a chubby little guy in wrap-around robes. There were also many who preferred to mix and match the prefix 'Zen' with the mystical aspects of one of the Western religions. Silence, laughter and dancing alternately dominated these gatherings.

Having presumed and thus activated their initial placements, all the Souls who had emerged from the tunnel that day finally prepared to settle in and rest. And rest is exactly what they needed — long, deep and reflective sleep, sleep that would help them answer the three major issues raised by their sudden appearance in the spiritual realm: Where exactly had they been and how did they get *here?* Was their presumed assessment and thus initial placement accurate? And, what had they contributed to the propagation of this thing called 'love' that the guides keep emphasizing?

Three days later — in Earthly terms, of course, since this was now the land of eternity - all the Souls who had recently returned from an incarnation would awaken to the news that it was now time to appear for their life reviews.

Amidst Friends

"Welcome, Danny," said the leader, a tall figure in the purple robes, seated at the opposite side of the round table. "We trust you slept well and are ready to join us in a review of the life you just completed on Earth."

"Sure," said Danny, nodding to the speaker and then glancing around the table at the others.

One person in particular caught his attention.

"Excuse me," he asked, 'but don't I know you from somewhere?"

"Yes," the cheerful female said. "I was your mother two incarnations ago."

"You've got to be kidding."

"No I am not. Let's face it — you've already picked up on the fact that we are connected in some way."

"And look there," she added, pointing to the shimmering image at the end of the row. "It's your brother, my husband, from three incarnations ago. And who do you think just guided you to your seat?"

"Sol?"

"The very same," said the plump male, "your old neighbor — in the flesh — so to speak."

"Are you sure I am still not sleeping — and dreaming the wildest dream I ever had? " said Danny. "This is the strangest — and most incredible place — I could ever imagine."

As soon as the laughter died down and introductions completed, the group got to work — but not before Danny walked around the room to shake hands and hug everyone at the table.

Danny had lived to be 64, been married twice, had three children, worked at a lot of different jobs, been in the service, and had interacted – like most – with thousands of people. His file was a thick one, for Danny had been involved in a number of situations which were of particular interest to the panel - including several high-wire dramas and some very memorable stories.

The first question was raised by the leader of the group: "Looking over your life, Danny, what makes you feel good?"

Danny smiled, bit his lip, muttered "oh my gawd", then puffed his cheeks, made funny noises with his mouth, straightened up and took a deep breath. Finally, he began to speak.

There was that fight at the bar, and the time he was fired (which was unjust because 'I took the rap for my cousin'). He also admitted to so-so grades in high school, and his arguments with his wives ('God rest their Souls'). He also noted his ambivalent feeling about working three jobs for years – but added that "I wanted the best for my kids: two of them, by the way, graduated from college and the other one owns a shopping center. Not bad, eh?"

"But there was my neglect of my religion," he said as a kind of confession, which he finalized later by "leaving the church totally: it just didn't make sense any more".

He both smiled and was a bit teary-eyed when he looked up after a long silence. "I guess I had by fondest feelings for my dog - 'Sanchez' - gawd, I loved that dog!" he said with a burst of enthusiasm. "And all the guys on the corner – ahh they were funniest bunch of guys ya'd ever meet. Of course we all went our own ways – but then we got together – like twenty years later – for a party that lasted for three days."

Danny looked up with tears in his eyes. His voice cracked. There was another a long silence.

"Sorry. There are so many things," he finally said. "At this stage I can't remember everything or be sure which things are important. I don't know. I guess I could've done better – in the education and marriage departments in particular."

"It's all crazy - yet it is all wonderful," he resumed. "Remember Holden Caulfield in 'Catcher in the Rye', one of the few books I ever read. I guess I was like him. No, no, no: I am like him! It was *all* worthwhile, if you know what I mean, and like Holden, I really miss everybody - including the jerk who fired me."

"How about a break, Danny?" said the leader of the panel in very soft tones. "It'll give us all an opportunity to stretch and move our energy fields around a bit."

"By the way," he asked. "How does it feel to not have a body to feed and lug around?"

"I'll tell ya right now," said Danny with a big grin. "I feel a lot lighter, that's for sure. Best diet I've ever been on."

Accenting the Positive

When the group reconvened, the leader introduced the next phase of the interview. "Allow us now to give you some feedback, Danny," he said, "feedback - regarding the life you just completed. Then – if you are willing - we would like to provide some guidance on issues you might want to look into when you proceed next to the Learning Lab and begin to think about what you want to do next."

"Sounds good," nodded Danny.

"Perhaps it would be best if each of us on the panel took turns – thus giving you a range of perspectives. You can then reflect on it all, see if you notice any patterns, and then initiate your own independent research at the Learning Lab."

"Judy. Would you like to get us started?"

"I would indeed. Remember, I was your mother two incarnations ago and I must admit my viewpoint is still tainted by that wonderful memory. You were a great student then and became a famous physician. I remember, one day when you were seven..."

"Judy," said the leader. "Danny's most recent incarnation, please."

"Oh lordy, yes. Thank you. Sorry. But, Danny, your successes two incarnations ago did have a lot to do with the choices you made in the most recent one. Even then you wanted to learn what it was like to be a working man with a blue collar job, to struggle with finances, to face the challenges of being a loving person despite facing some very trying circumstances."

"What strikes me most, in reviewing the details of this last incarnation, is how fair you were with everyone - despite the stress - including the man who fired you from that job you really loved, and the other guy who cheated you and the company you had just started. But you refused to seek any vengeance in the first case or to go to the authorities in the second. Pretty remarkable and commendable."

"Both of those guys had a wife and family," said Danny, "and I didn't want to hurt them the way each of them had hurt us."

"It is also true," she continued, "that you did not measure up to the standard you set for yourself in terms of listening and responding to the emotional needs of your own family. Your wife and children appreciated the income you earned through your hard work. But you overdid it. Overworking became a habit, a prideful one at that – like 'let's see how far I can stretch myself'. Working day and night thus became an easy way to avoid learning how to express your love - and your sorrow. It also became your excuse for not allowing yourself to be vulnerable and participate in a relationship of real depth."

"Gawd…damn, that's certainly right-on," said Danny under his breadth while thumping his right fist lightly on the table. He gazed up at the ceiling, put both hands on top of his head, sighed deeply and then slowly slumped forward. He tried to talk through his tears – but finally buried his head in his arms and allowed himself to cry.

There was a long silence.

"So," he finally asked, wiping his nose with the back of his hand. "Is this where hell comes in?"

The Common Good and Unconditional Love

"No", said another member of the panel - gently and with an understanding smile. "Forget all about hell and punishment. There is no such thing, and certainly not for the likes of you. Danny? Do you hear me?"

"Yes, I'm listening."

"Hell is something people create for themselves - on Earth - by being too hard on themselves and others. And punishment is self-inflicted – all those silly and at times cruel experiences people create for themselves if they don't sufficiently love themselves - and others. It sounds like you certainly created a living hell for yourself – at times, while you were on Earth. Now, however, that struggle is over. The memories linger only because they have something to teach you. You are home now, free from all that, and in a position to put it all into perspective, to learn from it and go on."

"In fact," said another member of the panel. "This may be a good time to summarize the divine system that exists here so you can put this review of your life in perspective. Can I take a few minutes?" he asked as he looked over at the leader, then Danny.

Both nodded, Danny adding an enthusiastic, "Yes. I am all ears!"

"What we are doing here - during this review - is raising the issues on which you wished to be assessed when you chose this last incarnation. We are merely the spokespeople for the progress you wished to make — as noted in the contract you drew up prior to your incarnation, the document that outlined your mission, your challenges and your living circumstances. Once on Earth, however, you had total free will to choose the details, the particulars that either fulfilled or negated your good intentions. It is those choices of those particulars that we are now reviewing."

"How are we doing," she asked Danny.

"Fine, fine. I am even taking notes!"

Contributing With Love

"Okay. Now, there are two major standards — one involves the expression of love and compassion, and the other focuses on making a creative contribution to the community. All Souls, by the way, choose to make at least some progress on both standards - including you in your most recent incarnation. Okay, so far?"

"Fine, fine, just — if you could - just talk a little bit slower."

"You got it," laughed the counselor. "I know: this is a lot but it is extremely important. You may have heard parts before but here it all is again in a nutshell."

"One aspect of any life, and thus relevant to all agreements for all incarnations — focuses on one's capacity to express unconditional love, the ability to love everyone and everything without exception or condition — that is, without any 'if onlys' or 'on condition that'."

"Now, unconditional love does not mean liking everything that happens or everything that all people do. But it does mean loving the deepest part, the Soul or core of your neighbor, your in-laws, strangers,

newcomers, any and everyone - as yourself — accepting and assisting them with the best of your loving intentions and support."

"The second constant in life - and thus also a standard for all incarnations — is how a Soul chooses to contribute to the common good. It is synonymous with service and productivity. Substantial or quality contributions can thus be made by anyone who intentionally commits to producing something of quality that others can use or from which they benefit. Such service can thus be rendered by anyone acting in any capacity — be it parent, friend, engineer, poet, mechanic, plumber and even a politician."

"Indirectly helping another while acting for purely selfish gain undercuts the potential value of the gift and thus does not really count. But doing something that flows from the intention to contribute to and serve the needs of others — in addition to oneself — certainly fits the bill, whether that contribution is an idea, invention, innovation, way of dealing with others, cure for polio, fixing a fence, baking a pie, building a bridge or even writing a book."

"These are difficult standards, we know," she concluded. "But they are the constant imperatives for all Souls. Loving as many people as often and unconditionally as you — while contributing to the common good as often as you can - are the two prime elements that personify Prime Source's love and support for each of us."

"Jesus and Buddha, of course - among many others - successfully mastered both standards. Most of us, however, have attained more modest goals. But with each incarnation, each Soul has the opportunity to continue learning how to love and how to contribute — more and more, person by person, situation by situation."

"So we are not here to judge you but to help you assess whether or not you learned what you wanted to achieve, whether you were able to fulfill the learning objections you selected, and whether you made the

progress you set for yourself - especially as it relates to the standards of unconditional love and making contributions."

"That's it," said the leader. "No more lectures! I hope this helps to put things into perspective. Thanks for listening. Now, back to the feedback and your responses."

The All-Important Particulars

"So," resumed Judy, "we are aware, for example, of all the allegedly small but very significant things you did during your most recent life on Earth: helping that man get on the bus after he had fallen, your trips to the hospital to visit your friends, your runs to the emergency ward in the middle of the night with one ailing child or another, the kind word you gave to a stranger that sat next to you at a diner — all unsolicited acts of love and joy."

"And," said still another member of the panel, "we realize you did not become a so-called professional — as you originally wanted. But who cares? You made all sorts of contributions to the common good, conducting yourself in ways that made life so much easier for your employees and colleagues. You modeled openness and innovation, and your boyish humor lightened the stress for everyone you worked with. You were also easy to forgive and forget when things went wrong, and you consistently rewarded people for quality service."

"You also learned to trust your loving instincts, either crossing the street, running across the aisles of a store, or getting up immediately from your table in a restaurant to instinctively aid somebody who was either ill, in need or incapacitated."

"And look here: in these last few years you learned to slow down, 'stopped to smell the roses' and even meditate. You prayed frequently and spontaneously - thereby helping countless numbers of people. And look at all the books on philosophy and spirituality you mastered, reading them on the bus and subway, sharing the books and their mes-

sages with family and friends. You were even known as 'the kindly philosopher' among your colleagues."

As the feedback continued around the table, the consensus was soon clear: Danny did not achieve all his goals, but most importantly he did love life, his children and friends. He extended help and a loving attitude to almost every one he met, and in the course of his varied careers made repeated creative contributions to the common good. On the debit side, he did not overcome something that has bothered him for several incarnations – namely, his fear and avoidance of personal intimacy. The need for money became his latest excuse for avoiding deeper emotional bonds with his wife and family.

"Yes I recognize the themes, and some of the examples," said Danny, shaking his head, "and I appreciate and accept the feedback. Learning about new ideas and how things operate is something I like to do. And, at least in a few cases, I learned something I have never been able to accomplish before – namely how to be a standup guy despite the provocation to do otherwise. But the personal intimacy issue is obviously still the big gap. So, in general, it seems I have made some progress but still have a long way to go. I guess that's why I'm now *here*. And that's why I intend to return *there* – that is, Earth - as soon as I complete a lot more soul-searching."

"Thank you," he said, wiping his handkerchief across his eyes. "I took a lot of notes and will keep them with me as I move *my studies* (I like that!) on over to the library in the Learning Lab. That is sure to help since - as I now recall - the Lab has all sorts of information not only on my checked lifetimes, but on every conceivable strategy on every issue - with lots of projections on the kinds of choices I could make for the future."

He stood, started to exit – but then turned around to face the panel.

"Wow," he said. "I am stunned and I am delighted. There is so much, so much to learn. And there - as I came through that tunnel - I

was sure I was finished: condemned - with my tail about to be burned. And now, here I am - appreciated for what I did accomplish, counseled on where I fell short, and encouraged to launch one more adventure. Obviously, I did die and go to heaven after-all."

Then She Heard Them Call Her Name

"Oh my," said the little and slightly older lady, as she watched Danny exit the counseling room. She had taken her hat off in a sign of respect and clutched it tightly next to her handbag.

Danny said hello as he passed her – then returned to ask if he could sit with her for a while.

"Oh, my, yes-yes, please do," said Wanda Granderson, moving slightly to one side so she could face him on the bench.

"I was gonna walk on by," confessed Danny, "but then took a chance, thinking we might both appreciate a little chat."

"Why that is very kind of you," said Wanda. "You are the first person without wings or dressed in a shimmering uniform to talk with me since I arrived. I admired all the folks here at the local heaven where they delivered me - but most seem preoccupied with their own importance. It's nice to have company."

Before Danny had a chance to respond, she confessed that she listened in on some of his chat with the elders.

"They said I could, in fact, they recommended it - to ease my nerves, I suspect. I hope you don't mind," she said with a smile, her eyebrows raised and a twinkle in her eyes. "It helped a lot, I mean I learned a lot – and got me remembering all sorts of things, like vague memories that I too have been here before."

"Well, tell me," she continued. "How was it? How do you feel after the big grilling?" she asked in a muted but deep voice, laughing at her imitation of James Cagney.

"Haw, it wasn't bad. In fact, as you heard, it was very helpful."

"Yes – they seem very nice - but I'm still scared. You see I now realize that I was the one who chose the challenges of my life - but I think I went too far. I sense I was a burly gangster of some sort, the time before – as you can probably tell from my imitation – so this time I wanted to be more withdrawn and polite."

"Well, withdrawn became timid, I am afraid - and politeness became my excuse for acting like a dried up old fuzzy. I did dance once in a while, alone in my own living room, of course. And I had a grand time with my dog Agatha until she died, poor thing. I never had any children, and although I bragged about all my nieces and nephews, I really did want a family of my own. I dated Charlie for years but by the time we got serious, I was unwilling and he was unable – if you know what I mean."

"Oh my," she continued. "I want to change a few things in my next life on Earth, if they let me have one." '

"Ah, sure they will," said Danny, nudging her on the arm, commenting that "choosing a new life, and incarnating where you wanted, seemed to be the way things operated – a tradition as old as the angels and as eternal as divinity itself."

"Well, you're probably right," answered Wanda, "and if so, I promise myself that in the next set of choices I want to stop saying 'oh my' and start learning how to use some daring words – maybe even a few off-color ones too. Come think of it, I might even learn to howl a bit - if you get my drift."

"I love it," said Danny laughing out loud. "Sort of a middle ground. Why not? You go for it, gal, you go for it. I'll be listening for you."

"I am sorry to admit that I was such a goody-goody all my life," concluded Wanda. "But I lacked energy, verve, the ability to be tough on behalf of the things I liked. I avoided conflict of any sort – and thus missed taking a stand for what I really wanted – all for fear of jeopardizing my safe little world."

"Fire and brimstone may be too much, but a pointy finger and a sharp tongue would have done me – and what I believed in – a world of good."

"What's that saying? 'Dance like there's nobody watching'. Yeah. That'll be me all right. A gen-u-ine risk taker. And maybe even a male risk-taker at that. I always liked Teddy Roosevelt."

Just then the door to the counseling room opened, and a melodious voice said: "Wanda, Wanda Granderson. Would you join us - please."

Facing Reality

As Wanda was repeating her life story to one panel, another panel was being formed to handle the other returnees. The first Souls they heard from were Edgar and Maude Simmons.

"Agnostic? Never even knew what it meant until I completed a few lifetimes as a cleric and then a high church official. So I figured I needed some balance and so signed on this lifetime as a prof at a secular college – hoping to learn something about rigorous dissent. Unfortunately, politics often outweighed the search for truth."

"Besides," he continued, " it took me ten years to shed the earlier smell of candles and the sight of black suits meeting in rooms where the curtains were always tightly drawn. And all that talk from the hierarchy about love – when all that seemed to matter was regulations,

control and cash. At least, as a secular I was more honest about being self-seeking."

Now *that* was Edgar's opening response to the question, "Please tell us something about yourself." The panel remained quiet – and attentive.

"It was only a bit different for me," said his wife, Maude. "I chose to become a teacher at a prestigious religious boarding school, neither clergyman or layman – if you catch my reference to gender. Then for emotional outlet, I came home to this austere soul who apparently loved to fondle nothing but books. Like a bird in a cage, I was: clipped, mollified, trained to mouth aphorisms on demand – a tight bundle of forced attributes that helped me attain acceptance on the job, and a bossy presence at home."

"Of course, it was no accident. I choose 'that very challenge' in this very room 76 years ago - thinking I could infuse manhood and emotion into someone like dear ole Edgar and yet still attain status as a female authority figure in a setting that had no precedence for such things. I obviously caved at several crucial junctures, finding I had neither the withal to lure Edgar into anything more sensual than afternoon tea, or the stamina to secure my place in a world dominated by men. Instead I became a bickering old fuddy-duddy; arrogant, suspicious and dreadfully lovely."

"Dearest, I do think you are again being too hard on yourself – and me as well," said Edgar with a force that startled her. "Together we stood up to a lot of silliness. We took risks. We were admired for our intellects. We stood alone against the world and poked it in the proverbial eye!"

"And what of the virtues we theoretically extolled - like love and kindness?" she retorted. "What of the philosophical virtues of modesty, forgiveness and attending to real people – versus our incessant need to protect our egos and pounce on the flaws in everyone else's appearance

and viewpoint. Notice how we reacted to that nice Luigi who greeted us at the gate. Huh: we showed him all right: nothing but disdain, suspicion and a shield of steel. And he still got us some hot coffee and even a Danish. Could be he really is an Angel."

"Do either of you remember Theresa — with whom you were close for while? Or Bart, an old colleague?" asked a member of the panel. "And then there was Georgette and Louis, the couple who lived across the hall."

"Oh, I regret ignoring Theresa, a good person at heart – but responding to her needs following the death of her husband was very inconvenient at the time," said Edgar. "To my regret, I respected only vigorous intellectual arguments that were presented with verve and daring. I am afraid my bloodless heart was threatened by people in real need."

"As to Bart, he was an emotional sort, always chatting with and even hugging his students, 'helping them to believe in themselves'," added Maude. "Oh, how I wished I could be like him – and each time I tried, I failed utterly. Students avoided me - and so I retreated to my world of ideas and laying in wait to challenge the assertions of others. Had I been stronger, I could have persevered with my original intentions. But in one case I chose the easy way out, and in the other, gloried in the alleged deprivation."

"And then there was Georgette and Louis," said Edgar. "A truly lovely couple," Maude added in a very low voice. "Helped us move, invited us in, shared their food and their library (such as it was), even loaned us money until we got on our feet following the car accident and our long stays in hospital."

"But, what did we do?" said Edgar, flapping his hands at his sides. "We reached the conclusion that they were mushy, overly caring. So we eventually and emphatically dropped them like a stone – and right after they had lost their youngest child."

"How ever did you dig up *these* people," asked Maude, and then quickly put up her hands in a sign of surrender. "We know, don't we dearest? It is evident in our perpetual frowns. All the stories reveal a continual theme: our minds overruled our hearts. We – individually and certainly together – showed a marked disinterest in anything but our ideas: high on the dry and the acidic, and very low on the sweet and enduring."

She began to cry. Edgar reached out his hand – then remained stiff and motionless. He pivoted gradually, moved closer, put one hand on her shoulder - his face lined with anguish. She said nothing, stared straight ahead – as if lost in her own thoughts.

Study, Learn, Design

Remember – how the five of us - Danny, Wanda, Edgar, Maude and I – exited the tunnel at approximately the same time, then lined up at the turnstile one behind the other, and thus entered through the celestial gate in close sequence. In the divine order of things, that clustering made for a convenient group – as we moved to the review panels and subsequently to the Learning Lab and all its opportunities for peer counseling.

The five of us chatted and shared quite often as we reviewed various past and present scenarios at the Lab. We also interacted socially at an endless variety of shows featuring whoever was in residence – or was passing through at that moment. Mozart, *the* Mozart – just back from his umpteenth incarnation, was the guest pianist one evening for his Symphony in C (his 41st). The star-studded audience included none other than Beethoven, Leonard Bernstein and Harry S. Truman. Dom Deloise entertained at the first intermission and Maria Callas and Allen Sherman sang a duet - of sorts - during the second break. It was the best of the best.

After long days in the Learning Lab, we greatly appreciated the evening entertainment – including a sing along (with you know who), listening to half of one of the big bands (the other half had moved on back to Earth), a question and answer session with Archangel Michael on the continuing evolution of the Kosmos, and dancing to the music of a series of stars from each of last five decades. By popular request, there was even a night of polkas and another featured tango lessons.

Primarily, however, we mediated and studied, and then reflected individually and collectively on what we had learned. The study tables and carrels at the Learning Center became our second homes. There were books, videos, televisions and computers everywhere. Most of our attention was initially focused on the records of our past lives and how those situations could have been changed with the selection of a different attitude, strategy or objective. Ah: the eternal present was indeed the best – and the safest place- for reviewing what is and could have been.

Decisions, Decisions

We then moved on to proposed scenarios for our next descent into the physical realm. There was so very much to consider. Setting high goals was good, of course, but being too ambitious could get us in trouble – again. That was the dilemma. Attaining wholeness, being of service, making contributions to the community, and learning how to love unconditionally were viewed not only as *the* desired goals but as very attainable goals.

But how much progress would we attempt this time? Didn't we try to do too much last time – or found our goals undercut by our susceptibility to temptation? Great visions are wonderful but they do need to be tempered by the hindsight we were now obtaining. Had we not already learned the realities of the material world - the hard way? Besides we were immortal Souls blessed with as much 'time' as it takes

to consolidate our gains. So we need not be in a hurry or become soul-centric by attempting too much, too soon.

In fact, we learned that a sufficient number of challenges to our goals were an essential part of any new learning contract; without them we could not prove our resolve and commitment. If learning how to express unconditional love was deemed to be a cakewalk, we would all be there by now. Aiming high but not too high: that seemed to be the right balance. Besides humility seemed closer to love than vanity and spiritual greed.

So we kept trying different scenarios for our next incarnation. All we had to do was type in a character trait, context and range of intentions, and the past or the potential opportunity and challenge would appear in 3-D on a life-size screen. Change any of the variables, and the cluster of probable outcomes would vary. If we also wanted to know what any of the situations or challenges actually felt like, then we could file a request for permission to enter into an event as a vivid, real-life experience.

We could even interview people from our past – a feat that was particularly easy if the Soul in question was then in residence. If the Soul had re-incarnated, then their Soul essences would become available for consultation during their dream state.

There were also a variety of fascinating counselors. Elves pinched and poked and encouraged laughter and good humor as they simultaneously invited us to put our dreams and concerns into drawings and paintings. Hobbits like Bilbo and Frodo led us through a set of hands-on explorations of what it felt like both to go beyond our comfort zones and experience the thrill of adventure.

The Fairies put on light shows to illuminate various vistas, and even urged us to 'lighten up' – physically and psychologically. And nature's Elementals – the representatives of earth, water, air and sun – demonstrated their respective virtues of non-judgment, spontaneity, cooperation, and using one's imagination.

Various birds and animals – including a three-legged deer - championed the joy of living in the moment. Former family and friends helped us recall what we may have wanted to forget. A rotating set of Angels took requests and delivered insights and wise counsel. And the periodic reappearance – and radiance - of an Archangel always motivated us to refocus on the basic decision of how much love, service and wholeness could we realistically achieve this next time around.

The key, of course, was to choose an outline of our desired patterns – our main contributions, trials, tribulations and joys. We were each getting close to making those major decisions but none of us was quite there as yet. Once those broad outlines were completed – our Guardian Angels advised us –then the details of such things as gender, parents, family, vocation and skill sets would fall into place.

Another Person Arrives

Unbeknown to the five of us, a sixth person had also entered the tunnel soon after us. Apparently he would have been included in our group had he not put up such a fuss en route to reentry.

Kenneth Oswald apparently refused to move through the tunnel once he saw the white light, and demanded he be sent back to Earth immediately. The guides told him that was not possible, at least not at that very moment.

Upon questioning and a preliminary check on his background, Kenneth admitted he had lots of nightmares recently while on Earth and feared being punished in retribution for what he called 'stupid allegations of alleged selfishness'. Given his expectations, the preliminary review, and the difficult time he gave even the most angelic of guides – he was finally asked to board a rickety old wagon that was parked down a very steep hill outside the main gathering area. It was slated to proceed immediately to a place called "Purge and Clean".

Reluctantly, Kenny finally stumbled down the hill, climbed aboard, and was soon delivered to the rickety old house several miles down a very dusty road filled with rocks and holes.

As soon as he entered the house – an old Victorian mansion like the one used in the movie, 'The Addams Family'– Kenny got in a fistfight with another resident regarding who called 'dibs' first on the large bedroom in the rear. It came as no surprise that the other guy – being a foot taller – got to claim the spot as his own.

There was nothing gracious about Kenny, however, who stayed up all night - exhausting himself and everyone else in repeated attempts to evict the other residents from their rooms. Finally, he did expel a paraplegic from his cot in the hall after scolding two children who came to the door begging for food. By morning he tried to romance one woman, then fell asleep in the arms of another who had the words, 'Me, Only Me', tattooed on her chest.

This pattern has been going on now for some time, Kenny turning what had been just a difficult house to one described as a 'living nightmare." Finally Kenneth S. Oswald was asked to appear before the review panel.

Sets of Choices

"Are you going back," Danny asked me.

"Eventually, yes, of course, I want to go return," I said. "I believe what the counselors say, namely that we all can learn to love - in still one more way, in one more situation. Facing the challenges of the material world seems to be the best way to achieve greater depth and experience."

"Oh yeah, the wholeness thing," said Danny. "So you want to return despite the fact that you've already lived on Earth for over 5,000 lifetimes?"

"Oh, yes, I want to go back," I stressed, "and this time I want to learn patience and helping people in distress, much as I hear you did. I would combine that with being a professional writer and evocateur – not for the glory (at least I hope to avoid that temptation) but for the sheer joy of being creative and encouraging others to realize their full potential. As to the particulars – parents, context, schooling, personality – I still have a lot of studying and choosing to do."

"Well, as you may know, if there is anything missing in what I have learned in my thousand or more incarnations," said Danny, "it's emotional depth. That means not only developing solid relationships but also learning how to share what is in my heart with whoever is willing to listen. Hey – get me with the big ideas! But, maybe, to seal the deal and give myself a head start, I might decide to return as a woman. The records suggest that more woman learn to love unconditionally - and faster – than the average man."

"Now you might think I am crazy, "but I also want to be a success, in my case, an architect, a first class one, designing creative yet intimate spaces."

"Of course," said Danny, extending his hands in an alternating rhythm, "we all need to include a set of losses and difficulties - problems that challenge our good intentions. No problems, no progress. Besides, we could still change our minds once we're actually on Earth. I hope we all do stay the course. But one thing we apparently can never relinquish is our free will. I will be as free to usurp my best intentions this time - as I was last time."

"Let's face it: we only choose the basic outlines here," he continued. "But down there we get to choose specifics - and some of them may fit and some may contradict what we agreed to in our Learning Contract. So even when we think we're ready and have chosen the terms of our new learning agreement, we still have the main work – the hard work - ahead of us, back down there on Earth."

And That Makes Four

"This may surprise you," said Edgar, "but I would like to be a nobody for a change. No titles, no pretensions, just a meat-and-potatoes kind of guy with a solid blue-collar job. Seems I've had very little empathy for such a lifestyle thus far. Perhaps it's about time I see how the other half actually lives. The change might make me more human. What do I want to learn? Now don't laugh: I want to learn how to be more practical, and I want to learn how to be more loving when it comes to interacting with people and handling life's everyday details with more passion."

"And," he said in a very low and hesitant voice, "I want to learn compassion by experiencing pain through a serious illness of my own. And I also want to learn what grief is like from the inside - by suffering the loss of a loved one."

"Being here has helped me understand that one of the best ways to learn how to deal with the realities of the world is to experience the realities of the world," Edgar concluded. "It the best way to break the pattern of aloofness and callousness I have exhibited for so many incarnations. I always descended with good intentions – some of my earlier Learning Contracts make me sound like Saint Francis. But I botched it all once it got to implementation. This time I know I need to learn a caring attitude since I have already decided to work with the dying in some future incarnation."

"Will wonders never cease?" laughed Maude. "Seems like this past lifetime was a positive undoing for both of us. Well, my dear and formerly frozen husband – who apparently now intends to meld into an absolute honey-bun – I'm headed for a dim and haunting spot light: a blues singer, a dancer, a red-hot momma who makes it from a cold water flat to fame and fortune on Broadway ... and brings a lot of good friends with her."

"Quite the change, eh?" she laughed. "But if we immortal Souls incarnate in order to eventually experience it all - then I might as well go where this ball of energy has never been before, and then risk it all in one wild and wonderful incarnation."

Wanda listened intently to all these testimonies and promises – then began to draw on large sheets of paper with the set of colored markers she found on the desk. On one sheet she had written 'scared', 'confused' and 'hopeful' - words that she thought described what all of us experienced when we first came through the turnstile.

"But look at the words that now seem to summarize our new intentions," she said as she took out a second sheet. On it she scrawled 'empowerment' in red, then 'choice' in green, 'trust' in orange and 'compassion' in deep purple and outlined in gold.

"And look here", she shouted gleefully: I just wrote down the words, 'Create' and 'Contribute, and the phrase, 'Unique – Thus Contributing to My Community'. I was inspired by the session we had with Archangel Gabriel: creation is continuous and we are its agents – always signing on for one more enlightening experience, always returning to tell God all about it, always delighting in the adjustments He then makes as the universe evolves en masse toward greater degrees of love and compassion."

Danny said he particularly liked her colored set of circles – which looked like facets of a spiral. Some of the green rings seemed to spiral inward, deeper and deeper in a counter clock-wise motion. Others – a rich red - looked like they were reaching up and out. And each of the rings was covered with differently colored hearts.

"That's us, all right" said Maude. "Individually and together: growing internally and then expressing it outwardly. Maybe *that's* what makes for 'wholeness," she exclaimed - her eyes bright, her head bobbing up and down. "Besides," she said, "there will always be new ways and new worlds - to create and discover."

"There will always new ways and new worlds – to create and discover."

Purge and Clean

The interview did not go well.

Even the first question, "Looking over your life, what makes you feel good?" – elicited a sour response.

"Good?" said Kenny, with a sneer on his face. "Come on. Assuming you people mean well, this is all pretty silly. You have no jurisdiction. You know nothing about me. And you can't keep me in that rat house you call a 'temporary accommodation' – forever. I aspire to something much better, regal perhaps."

"Let's start again, shall we," said the panel leader in a soft voice. "Even if what you say is true, you are here now – so why not at least take this opportunity to comment on anything that made you feel good during your last experience on Earth."

"Right," said Kenny. "Well I was a first-rate engineer but most of the firms I worked for did not appreciate me. So I left. F — k 'em."

"I was married, had a few affairs – that really bothered her, so I was divorced, remarried, had a few more flings – and that also bothered each one of them. All I ever wanted was to live a good life – and all I got was complaints and nagging."

"And the kids? I bought them stuff but it was never enough. They wanted something their mother taught them to say, namely 'Quality Time' – whatever that is. What am I, a renaissance man? I paid the bills, didn't I - more than some guys do. After a while I realized the visitations were not worth it: traveling, scheduling, more expense – and boring too."

"I enjoyed some of my co-workers – especially the ones I dated," he said with a big laugh. "Compete, win-lose, outfox the other guy – a lot like the rat hole you put me in. Nobody is really your friend. Everyone is a potential enemy – and you might as well strike first and protect yourself."

"Do you feel you have been responsible for causing or generating any of the difficulties you describe?" asked a member of the panel.

"People get what they deserve," Kenny responded quickly.

And on and on it went, until the group convened and the panel met in private conversation.

Upon their return, the leader of the counseling group made the following statements:

"We do not judge you, Mr. Oswald. We are here to counsel you, do what we can to make you aware of your choices, and then help

you face the consequences of those choices. Unfortunately, you do not yet exhibit any desire to learn from your experience or accept responsibility for the considerable harm you have caused yourself and others."

"We therefore ask that you attend a series of counseling sessions, and begin using our Learning Laboratory to review the impact of your past decisions. We also ask you to remain at what you refer to the 'rat-hole' until you have learned to empathize with and thus take responsibility for the harm you created for others – now at the Mansion, but especially during your last incarnation. In other words, this is your opportunity to experience directly the kind of demeaning and harmful thoughts, emotions and actions you perpetrated on others. If you wish to change any of that experience, you might consider your current placement as the perfect place to begin your conversion."

"You will also be given the opportunity – for as long as it takes – to learn how to convert those harmful situations into experiences that create awareness, responsibility and love," the leader concluded. "If at any juncture you wish to consider your range of options – up front and personal, so to speak - you may want to participate in our ReEnactment Theater. Details will be made available upon request."

"In conclusion, we encourage you to work on bolstering your core identity as an immortal Soul. Should you choose to do the work on yourself that this panel deems essential, then you can slowly but clearly earn your way out of your recurring predicaments. If not, then you may condemn yourself to long-term residence at the Mansion as well as a continuing set of catastrophes should you ever venture back to Earth."

"Like everything else in the universe, what you experience depends on the choices you make and the circumstances you then attract that mirror and confirm your attitude and intentions. Think anger and act out of a sense of deprivation and you will surely fulfill those prophecies.

Intend love and act with compassion and the same energies will rebound to you a hundredfold. We wish you the latter, and only hope that — sooner or later - you do as well."

"Should you wish to discuss your situation, or need any of us for any reason, ring the gong that sits on the porch of your current residence, and one of us will be happy to respond."

"Do you have any questions?"

Kenny, rocked gently in place, hands clasped loosely at his waist, and for the first time in weeks, stood mute.

A Different Tunnel, A New Beginning

"Whish, splash — at ease, rocking like a boat - here in the bay of bliss. No care, no worry — only an increasing need to stretch."

"Hmm — what's this? Moved my foot and for the first time it pushed against something. It was soft and forgiving but it suggests there is a container out there."

"And - oh, that was a real bump: gave it the old hip. Felt good. I was getting lonely for someone to play with. The cord has been fun but it doesn't exactly do anything. Oh, wait a minute: I can see a toe. Now it feels like I'm bending and stretching at the same time. What is going on?"

"Suddenly something is pushing on my rear end. Hey — that was a real shove. There's another, and another. It seems I'm on the move. Going faster. See some light. I am tumbling toward it. Golly but the space is tight. Will I fit?"

"Another long tunnel: vague memories. No gates, turnstiles or queuing this time. The lovely person in radiant outline has been replaced by an all-white monster wearing a mask and gloves."

"Blinding light, sounds of music, cries of 'yes, yes', long fingers, big hands, snip-snip."

"'Oh my, it's my baby,' someone cries."

"Suddenly I am vertical, literally up side down, held by the ankles."

"*Zow! That whack is not exactly my idea of a greeting.*"

"*Now I'm being a wrapped, set in a cradle. Gradually, finally – I doze off. Then suddenly I awaken to softness, a nipple, ah – milk. I hold on as I long as I can – then doze off again into a deep, deep sleep.*"

"*With each snooze, I sense a relinquishing of memory – a fading sense of who I am and where I came from. I catch a glimpse of Nathaniel, hear his voice: 'we are with you always.' Then both this outline and his voice - fade.*"

"*But where are my friends, my core group - and all the others! Where have they gone? What happened to Danny? And Wanda? Will we met again? Oh, please remember me, please remember my story.*"

"*And God – oh God: I do not feel your presence as I did at the Learning Center*".

"*Now - here comes the outline of another person, one with a large eye and very soft and soothing voice.*"

"*I smell scented lotion.*"

"*Incredible: is this new face, this smiling face – also divine?*"

As The Years Passed

I have lived many years now, 74 to be exact. It is the age when I go to more funerals than baptisms, when the passing of the body has become a glaring reality. I am losing a friend here, a colleague there, and recently my good neighbor, Frank, and dear friend, Sam.

The holidays have become a way of keeping count – as to who has the most grandchildren and whose absence or silence indicates they have passed on.

I don't feel death is imminent or near for I am in excellent health and have always nurtured the sense that I will not relinquish this particular body until I am into my hundreds – 103 to be exact, maybe even 106 if something exciting is still going on.

So I have approximately another thirty years in this incarnation. I've completed the usual epochal events – gained independence from my family of birth, had lots of formal education, married, had children, pursued a few different careers, tussled with my birth-church, and traveled and puttered around here and there. So the question becomes: what will I do next with the time I have remaining? And will I make any of it count in terms of the promises I made this time just prior to re-incarnating again on Earth?

I certainly have more time now to pray and meditate, to walk in the woods and commune with Mother Nature, to attend to my family and now six grandchildren, and especially think of and write about the issues raised in this story.

The details escape me but my day and night dreams continue to stir memories of a purely spiritual realm - where radiant figures teach and guide, and where both old and new friends continually reappear as if it was yesterday. Challenges to be more loving and opportunities to contribute continue to emerge – seemingly every day and in every situation here on Earth. Yet increasingly they are informed by glimpses of other lives, and realms that seem everlasting.

Glimpses

Many of my current thoughts and explorations stem from a series of interactions I had over the years: conversations I recall, chance meetings that made me wonder, sets of coincidences that – as today's youth say – 'rocked my world.'

Years ago – while kneeling in a church in Italy, for example - I straightened up to let a woman go by. As she passed, she turned and

asked if I had dropped the paper she had in her hand. I don't think so, I replied, but took the material and examined it more closely.

Had I dropped it? Was it mine? Perhaps I should return it? As I turned I noticed the entire pew was empty and the woman was gone. But next to me was a free-lance drawing of an artistic center. Turning the paper over I discovered the half sentence: ''Love your creative work-shops and books.'

Then there was the pamphlet that suddenly fell from the stacks as I perused a little bookstore in London. I picked it up as I heard a bell ring. I looked up: one had been fastened to the top of the front door. A woman with a large, colorful hat was at the doorway. She waved, turned, and disappeared into the night. The book was entitled, "Your Red Hot Momma."

On another occasion, I overhead a conversation that sounded like one workman telling another how to lay bricks. "Empower your trowel," he said. "And instill some passion as you tap down the mortar."

I laughed and walked around the truck that was blocking my view. There was a trowel lying on the ground. No a wheel barrel, no pile of bricks, not even the hint of a wall. The space was empty. I looked around and even called out. Silence: absolute silence.

Funny, silly coincidences, many say. It could happen any time to any one. But you can also view them as signs of other dimensions at work, spiritual moments that link the timeless past with the fleeting moments of the present, the mundane and the other side interwoven, reminders that we are connected, here, there and everywhere, all of it impossible yet all of it real.

I have heard all the disclaimers and denials a hundred times. But I know what happened, and can vividly recall the circumstances. Even now, I can relive the sense of energy and confirmation created by each of those events. I do not recall the details of what occurred in the spiritual realm that caused these earthly 'coincidences' to occur and

resonate so deeply. Total recall of what happened in the spirit world would – undoubtedly - make it all too easy to live a responsible spiritual life back here on Earth. And it would surely negate the work involved in learning how to affirm the constancy of the spiritual domain despite the absence of what others consider clear and undeniable proof.

But I do know - in the deepest part of me - that such experiences stem from a connection I had with a team of others prior to my being born - his time - three quarters of a century ago. I also sense on-going agreement among the members of our little group to be of help to each other. If we weakened in one of our major commitments, for example, one or more of the others would initiate an encounter that communicated their continuing presence and support. Each of the disguised 'visits' I experienced did have a great impact: they encouraged me to Soul-search all the more, review my intentions and actions to date, and redouble my efforts to act like the immortal Soul I am – one that is on a self-proclaimed mission to contribute what I can, while I can.

Often I am aware as well of being coaxed and even beckoned – as if an angelic being hovered near me, offering guidance on how to treat myself - and others - with just a little more love and understanding.

Oh, oh: let us not forget the incident of the spirals. Several years ago I was literally bombarded – intermittently for months - by the sighting and receipt of spirals: big ones appeared on a billboard in Western New York, three smaller ones arrived from the children of friends following my heart surgery, one of my grandsons gave me another as part of a birthday gift, and six more decorated with hearts arrived in the mail – with no forwarding address; three green spirals circled inward while the red ones arced out to the edge of the paper.

I have also had a recurring dream of an old house gradually being transformed into a joyful and palatial home. And recently while attending a play in New York City, I returned from intermission to find an envelope on my seat. Inside was a sheet of paper on which the phrase 'Unconditional Love' had been spelled out using such symbols of set

design as lights, curtains, home furnishings and power tools. No name, no signature - only slight smudges of glue.

Each time I am reminded of real but invisible friendships, each time I receive an inkling that the world is alive with loving spirits, each time I am reminded of my spiritual identity, I feel gifted and protected and oh-so fortunate and blessed. Such experiences are almost impossible to explain but I am sure they emanate from the spirit realm – that glorious place where the grids are drawn and riverbeds are contoured, where the fabric of the universe was once carefully created, and where it has, ever since, been updated and adjusted with a very knowing, loving and gentle touch.

Somebody Rang the Gong

Apparently, the difficulties that had been experienced earlier down at the old Victorian Mansion continued unabated – lasting for what some felt was the better part of a lifetime. The fights, the screams, the incessant bouts of crying, all seemed to prove that it was indeed the place of *Purge and Clean*.

Then one bright and shiny day, the turmoil died down – but there was still a lot of activity going on in and around the house. For example, there were reports of someone bequeathing a cot to another resident. Apparently, its long-time user had even washed the sheets and bought a supportive mattress before handing it over – in a prayerful ceremony no less – to a beggar who had been living in a corner of the cellar. Soon after, the donor vacated the house and chose a spot out back so he could sleep in his words, "under the stars - in a handmade tent".

A few days later, somebody rang the gong. It startled everyone. Who? What? When? Why? No answers. A delegation of angels came by, discussions were held, and promises were made. Sensitivity toward others seemed to be the major theme. Before long, however, the

tension was back, shoes were flung, doors slammed, and arguments lasted through the night. Strangely, however, things were quiet in and around the tent.

Not long thereafter, the gong rang again, apparently after the camper had reentered the house and raised hell about the 'merits of heaven' and how folks were wasting their lives.

Soon the residents of the house were seen sharing a meal together. Then somebody was seen repairing the roof and fixing the front stairs. There was even the smell of paint. And then, lo and below, a notice was distributed to everyone in the area: come Sunday, there was going to be a gala party thrown for the neighborhood children.

Back to Basics

The rickety old wagon that serviced the dilapidated old Victorian Mansion arrived one day with three new residents. As they unloaded their things, another Soul, carrying only an old army duffle bag, boarded for the return ride.

Beginning with the very next sunrise, the number of files and videos being used in the Learning Lab increased markedly. A huge pile of opened books was also being assembled in the large carrel on the second floor. On it someone had made a sign constructed from cutouts of colored paper. Using an assortment of geometric figures and symbols, the message read: "Please-Please - do NOT disturb. A Loving and Significant Project in Process". Around the same time, a tent went up outside – just to the left of the main door.

The furnishings in the ReEnactment Theater were also being used at a record pace. Volunteer players, lighting specialists and scenery designers were quickly volunteering to accommodate the newest playwright, a relatively young and somewhat tattered-looking male who apparently was on a mission to right some wrongs.

Initially, everything the newcomer presented was a tragedy – plays on the ancient themes of pride, ego and catastrophe: scary, ghastly, really sad stuff, filled with lots of shouting, cursing and wailing.

Then slowly the mood shifted, and the would-be playwright would arrive from the Learning Center with totally different kinds of scripts. The string of tragedies that once flowed unceasingly from his pen, were now to be shelved, he said: "they were no longer descriptive of either my past or any part of the reality I wish to create."

The catharsis apparently was over. "I can and will take responsibility," he affirmed with a broad smile. "I now want to create adventures, participate in a comedy, maybe even play a supportive – or lead - role in a lovely romance."

Of course, the opportunity to enact such a varied repertoire delighted the rotating sets of directors, crews and players - each of who, on various occasions, had also been residents of the now infamous Mansion. Earlier, such an affiliation, if known, generated sophisticated forms of shunning, especially by those who had chosen to live in one of the self-created heavens. But smiles, laced with surprise and then begrudging applause slowly became the norm - that is until the arrival of the season's final production.

The stage production of "One Man's Change of Heart" was greeted with such acclaim and attracted such huge audiences that it ran for several weeks. New scenes were added, and appreciative audiences kept extending its run. As reported in the *Pure Spirit Gazette*, the expanding community effort now featured a cast and crew that would have made Cecil B proud.

And the resultant saga so intrigued and stimulated everyone associated with the production that it made them, in the words of the reviewer, "keenly aware that the loving lifelines they were designing could potentially rock the agenda – and the psychological orbit - of the entire planet Earth."

A Last Word – For Now

Obviously, the many people involved in this production – playwright, directors and crew – were becoming increasingly aware that there were no constraints on what they could wish to accomplish – as long as they mustered the will and the love needed to realize their lofty goals.

"Remember," said the Spirit Guides at the Lab and Theater: "Whatever you choose to do, be sure it is energized by the desire to contribute and the intention to love. If so, the individual and the community will inevitably reach wholeness and unity with Prime Source."

"If not," they emphasized, "you and your mission could backslide – and they will if your Souls are overwhelmed by silliness and selfishness – a event that could set off an endless cycle of tunnels and gateways, rides on a rickety old wagon and long stays at a rundown old Mansion."

"Not to worry," said the new playwright. "The latest script and set design combines the best insights and constructive energies of many, many Souls – some of us with tainted pasts, we admit - but all of us now sharing a greatly inspired perspective, one that will – with God's help - enable us to attain the goals of our humble yet heroic epic."

The community was hushed in silence – whether in disbelief or reverence for what they were hearing. No one had talked this way in many an incarnation. It echoed the intentions of earlier avatars, saints and mystics whose names are now emblazoned on Earth's otherwise mixed reviews on achieving love and compassion.

"Will this be the making of another advance for our war-torn planet?" many Souls asked. "Can this former occupant of 'Purge and Clean' sustain his commitment?" wondered his Guardian Angel. "Had the old Mansion worked its wonders after all?" smiled Luigi, the angel posted at the gate opposite the tunnel.

"We assure you," the playwright continued, speaking directly now to the assembled group of Angels, "the combined efforts of our small but dedicated community will not disappoint God or the Angelic Hierarchy. Our loving intent is pure and our commitment to instilling compassion throughout Mother Earth is both unshakeable and achievable."

"When we inevitably re-emerge from that tunnel," he emphasized, "we trust that our Life Review will not warrant being reassigned to the Victorian Mansion – at least as it is now constituted."

"In fact," he added quickly, "many of us upon our return here wish to convert the old Mansion into a glorious home - one with both quiet and community rooms, a place where all can share and all are welcome, a huge home with all sorts of individual and unique nooks and crannies, where each spot also has instant entry to all the other sacred spaces, the totality being - in essence – a true 'Heaven'."

"If so," he concluded, "such a home would serve the increasing number of returning Souls who – given their service to God – would never need to incarnate again. Having personified the standard of unconditional love, they will have earned the right to reside here for all eternity."

"Of course," he said with a broad grin, "God may still need such elevated Souls for special assignment, and they may very well be among the first to volunteer."

"But that is another story – one that is beyond our spirit grade. But, who knows," he said with a twinkle in his eye. "Maybe God will let all of us help Her complete the set designs for those projects too?"

The assembled souls and angels applauded the resolve of the playwright and his compatriots – bowing to them, throwing them kisses, shouting out wishes of love. Spontaneously, all paused in prayer, asking that God bless the playwright and empower him to attain on Earth that which was always glorified in Heaven. Would mind and spirit be

---

united again, they wondered, somewhere if not everywhere on Earth? Was it not time for a new avatar to teach the world how to love, for the false veils to fall again and the divide fully healed at last?

They bowed as the playwright entered the tunnel, waved and cheered as he cleared the other side of the tunnel - then made his descent, fulfilling his choice to enter again into the earliest stages of a newborn.

His colleagues, of course, promised to follow in agreed stages. It was not surprising, of course, that Danny and Wanda also chose immediately to join the queue. Maude and Edgar - and I – thought it best, however, to stay a bit longer. We knew we would soon incarnate again as well, but we also accepted the fact, at the time, that we still had some work to do on that other side.

"Believe me," said Danny as he reentered the tunnel en route to his latest incarnation: "Once any of us remembers who we *really* are – namely, an immortal Soul - then choosing 'love and compassion' becomes the most natural, the most joyful and most fulfilling thing we can do."

Since then, we too have obviously descended and are now in the midst of fulfilling our promises for another lifetime on Earth. In the meantime, staying in touch with each other – indirectly through our notes and walk-bys – has been incredibly nourishing. Each glimpse, hint and recall acts like a dose of spiritual energy, and keeps me – and I am sure, all of us – deeply aware of our spiritual identity.

Angels At Work

Miracles Unfold As Humans and Angels Unite

It is one big, cosmic cooperative team.

First, humans learn to invoke the assistance

of their Guardian Angels.

The Angels – who are in training - then turn to

Archangels Gabriel, Raphael and Michael

to invoke their loving, healing and protective energies.

Thus you would not be surprised to learn that

this triple-tiered cooperative of humans, angels and Archangels,

then proceeds to create a series of wondrous miracles

all of which are ultimately affirmed and blessed

by none other than Prime Source Herself.

Angels in Training

"It's boring it is to sit here on the edge of this cloud, just waiting for any of them to call."

"How long have you been sitting here?"

"In their human time: about a year. But in our time – only a few seconds. But so much is going on. Charlie and Edna have argued and

now parted, little Harry doesn't know what to do with the bully who corners him every day, Sally feels she needs to act dumb in class or the boys will tease her…on and on and on. Yet none call on me."

"Did that priest ever call, or the Pope, or that woman in that collapsing house on the hill?"

"Nope."

"Ever hear from that brilliant prof with the drinking problem or the minister who fears he's lost his faith?"

"Not a word."

"How about that unemployed mother who was deserted by her boyfriend?"

The other Angel just frowned.

"And the mean farmer forced to sell the family farm, and the newborn who discovered the realities of living with parents who fight all day? Don't tell me they haven't called either. How much difficulty do they need before they realize there is an alternative to toughing it out on their own?"

"No …no … nothing … and nada," said Antonio. "Like every angel up here, I'm ready to help - but the incarnated Souls below don't seem to realize that all they need to do is call."

"They've got phones, and computers, Google, tweeting, texting, and e-mail to contact whoever they want on Earth for any consolation or information they need. In fact, they're the most consoled and informed generation that planet has ever supported. But they have yet to learn that none of that works very well - or for very long."

"With all those substitutes now on hand, they've obviously forgotten how to pray, or meditate, or invoke God's assistance with the simplest of words and intentions. The result: the chatter down there is incessant and at an all time high - while the airwaves reaching us go unused."

"Just look at how many Angels are sitting around," Sarah said with a wave of her left wing. "It's such a waste. Our human charges remain miserable and we remain unemployed. What's an Angel to do?"

Gabriel Hears Them

Archangel Gabriel was concerned too. So was his sidekick, Raphael, who along with Michael will soon play crucial roles in our story.

Let's first say a few words about Gabriel since he was the first of the Archangels created by God many eons ago to help handle one of God's most innovative creations. That innovation, of course, was the creation of the billions of Souls who since choose periodically to inhabit what has come to be known as the physical universe.

Gabriel's purview has always been enormous, stretching from the black holes of deep outer space to the everyday concerns of the many Souls who - in order to deepen their spiritual experience - continue to incarnate on such planets as Earth. Gradually, however, Gabriel's energy became increasingly focused around the empowerment we know as communicating, counseling and guiding. He is, for example, a teacher par excellence - perfectly capable of inviting you, nudging you, whispering in your ear, creating a so-called coincidence or arriving personally to annunciate or remind a Soul of its true ministry or mission.

So life is never dull for this literal ball of energy - as he splits his near infinite attention across millions of light-years of time and space. He is like a cosmic Plastic Man, capable of manifesting as the wisp of the wind, a very tall and imposing human figure, a winged Angel, a slice of brilliant light or one of those sprawling Cirrus clouds that spreads its features over half the sky.

Invoke Gabriel's – or any Angel's energy – or ask them a question or for advice – on anything – and they are sure to answer you either in

a dream, a coincidental 'happening', a sudden awareness or an intuitive insight.

Angels are most likely to stimulate an insight, however, after we proactively request it or display a marked receptivity to their presence. Thus insights are most often gifted during – or shortly after - prayer and meditation. It would be presumptuous, however, to expect the guidance they send to be exactly like one we wanted to receive; getting what we ask for often is not always in our best interest. As to timing and our desires for instant miracles: remember our year is but a nano-second in eternity.

We tend to refer to Gabriel as 'he". Gabriel, or any Angel, could just as easily be 'she' or 'it' – since Angels, like God, are total beings, beyond gender, perfect combinations of what we on Earth refer to as the psychological traits of male and female. They are pure blends of assertiveness and receptivity, the rational and intuitive approaches to life. The designation of "It" would probably be the most accurate but 'it' sounds a bit cold and aloof. So, for convenience, we'll stay with tradition and attribute a gender to each of the Angels.

Given the incredible range of *his* powers, Gabriel – as an Archangel – could, at this very instant, be preventing a collision of galaxies at the outer edge of the universe, transplanting life to a new planet in Andromeda, sending out messages of love to the citizens of several planetary systems, helping an earthly businessman learn how to meditate, blessing an female minister in San Francisco, and assisting a young couple assemble the rent due on their apartment in Mobile, Alabama. Gabriel – like each of the Archangels - is 'big po'aters', as they say in Ireland - very big indeed.

"Teacher, guide, facilitator, prod and provocateur - are among the many skills and characteristics of Archangel Gabriel."

To Annunciate

But 'big' does not really explain what Gabriel does most - and best. As noted, he is primarily a guide who both empowers and encourages people to use their skills, optimize their potential, and commit to realizing their chosen mission in life.

For example, remember the biblical story of the Annunciation in which God sends Gabriel to inform Mary that she is pregnant with a divine child. Whether you translate the Bible literally or figuratively, the process of annunciating is - at a minimum - a wondrous metaphor, indicating how Prime Source uses the first of *His* (there we go again) Archangels to activate our inherent power to create.

To *annunciate*, then, is to activate a creation, to encourage the *birthing* – of a child or a personal calling, an idea or organization, a career skill, a loving attitude or a courageous undertaking. Annunciating helps to activate whatever a person has chosen to accomplish while on Earth. It kick-starts implementation of the focus each of us chose when we 'descended' from the realm of Pure Spirit and assumed a physical or incarnated form on Earth.

Whenever any of us feels the urge to create - to express or attain some personal skill, professional capacity or contribution to the community - there will be Gabriel, encouraging us to give concrete form to whatever we have chosen as our intended contribution. It is thus Gabriel's mission to help us heed God's continuous call to create, and serve, and contribute - to our own development as well that which is our community and thus the continuous creation of the universe itself.

Gabriel is also known as Benu, an ancient Egyptian term meaning 'door' or 'passage-way' – the means for converting intention into expression, an image to implementation, an idea into an actual innovation. This is the energy that causes Muslims to appreciate Gabriel for his

dictating the Koran to Mohammed, Jews to extol him for encouraging Daniel to believe in the coming of a Messiah, and Christians to love him for delivering God's message to Mary that she would conceive and give birth to Jesus.

Teacher, guide, facilitator, prod and provocateur - are among the many skills and characteristics of Archangel Gabriel. He is often depicted carrying a stem of flowers to indicate the intent to serve and the impulse to create. Small wonder, then, that it is Gabriel who happens to wander by as our two Guardian Angels twiddle their thumbs and anticipate another three-day holiday.

Teacher and Trainees

"Good evening, my friends," said Gabriel. "Something troubling you?"

The radiance of the newcomer was brighter than anything the two Angels had ever seen — that is, since the time they received their commissions from the Council to become Guardian Angels in Training (or GAIT for short). They also noticed they were gradually being enveloped by a new and very strong field of light energy — one that made them vibrate as well — and at a high frequency.

"Is that you, Lord?" asked Sarah, as she and her partner scrambled to full attention.

"No, no - it is only me," said the Archangel. "Gabriel at your service."

"My word - and with all due respect - what, may we ask, brings the likes of Archangel Gabriel to the edge of this everyday and out-of-the-way cloud?"

"Oh, let's just say I heard you talking as I entered Earth's orbit and it sounded like you could use a pep-talk."

"Pep talk? How to handle the 'no talk' from below would be more like it," said Antonio, who, although usually shy — suddenly felt enlivened.

"Ah, now that's more like it,' said a smiling Gabriel. "Is that an explicit request for help?"

"Yes - it is," Sarah and Antonio muttered simultaneously — as they looked at each other and laughed.

"Ah: now you know what it's also like for me - waiting for you, and almost all of the Guardian Angels — in training or fully commissioned - to ask me and my colleagues for help. Just because you've working on your GA degrees does not mean you have to figure everything out on your own. Forgive me if I poke you a bit, but I heard you complaining loud and clear as I rounded Saturn. But I have never heard either of you utter a direct request for assistance."

The two Angels nodded sheepishly ... then laughed - realizing that they, like their human charges, complained to each other but were mum when it came to asking for divine assistance. Handling life on one's own — as an incarnated Soul or an Angel - is certainly a virtue and a builder of character. But assuming one no longer needs God's help, or that you had to be on your own once you chose your assignment — was both untrue and silly. Listen to how Gabriel explained the process of universal partnership.

The Universal Partnership

"Forgive me, please, if I transit into my teaching role for a few minutes," said Gabriel, "and say a few things about helping relationships. I prefer question and answer sessions, but given your relative silence — and now receptivity — I hope you don't mind if I lecture a bit."

The two Angels in Training just smiled, anxious to receive Gabriel's insights yet hoping his words would be succinct and immediately useful.

"First, you are certainly right," he began. "You cannot force yourselves on your human charges any more that I can force myself on you. Most don't even know that Angels exit – because they have no idea there is such a thing as God's legion of counselors. And many people only recognize God as a desirable but vague concept. They simply have not bowed their heads often or deep enough to experience Him directly and know that He and his divine forces are available every second of everyday."

"These wondrous Souls that you seek to guide have – of course - again chosen to re-incarnate on Earth – choosing one more lifetime in the material realm in order to further develop their spiritual capacities. But no single reincarnation is easy or self-executing. Re-incarnated Souls occasionally have an inkling of who they are - namely spiritual beings having another Earthly experience. But while in the physical realm they are not allowed to recall the fullness of their immortal identity – lest the challenges they chose to face while on Earth became little more than walks in the park."

"Help is always available, to all of us - as you well know," said Gabriel, "but rather than creating love and infusing spirit into the Earth, the human ego can get inflated, think it is both alone and totally in charge, and to varying degrees, divert its capacity to create love into power-seeking ventures and the pursuit of personal gain."

"So, the immediate needs of the ego can assume command and overwhelm the intentions of the Soul, not all the time necessarily, but often enough to prevent the Soul from exercising its sacred powers and achieving its divine mission."

"In the process, the incarnated Soul tends to forget all about us," said Antonio. "It takes a disaster before any of them finally turn to us – no less to God. Only then, when one of them is hanging onto a cliff by their fingernails - do we ever get a call."

"In the meantime, how much poker can a Guardian Angel play? We might have to open an agency to help unemployed Guardians," said Sarah – her outline fluttering from her laughter.

"Does that mean you're now asking for help on how to deal with your human charges?" asked Gabriel.

"Well, it definitely does," said Sarah, again exchanging glances with Antonio. Then they both nodded sheepishly. "Absolutely," said one. "By all means," affirmed the other.

Responding to Calls for Assistance

"You cannot save a person, that is, do their work of them," Gabriel continued. "That is divine law. But you can and are expected to assist when any one of three circumstances arise. Let me take just another minute to explain."

"First, some people finally stop stalling and make a clear and direct request for assistance. Although even these are rare, they are clearly discernible. Message sent, message received."

"Second, there is the kind of request that is so muted you can hardly hear it — but it is still real. For example, I sense you are waiting to be shouted at or your wings pulled. But human requests for help are often indirect — as in a string of muted prayers. If repeated, those muffled outcries can indicate sufficient openness and receptivity. When they accumulate, it is time to intervene and respond."

"Third," said Gabriel, as he adjusted his energy field to a low shimmer, "some humans associate asking for assistance with surrendering their independence. They have an especially difficult time, under any circumstance, displaying any so-called 'weakness' — even to their family and friends — no less to the likes of us who are totally invisible to most of them, most of the time."

"But…but," he said with emphasis, "there comes a time when — in near desperation — such people finally do cry out. It is like a foxhole conversion. They give up on grumbling, feel so alone and in so much pain that they just surrender their prideful resistance. These people

may take a while but when you hear from them they are as loud and clear as can be. Think of Scrooge in 'The Christmas Carol'."

"So," Gabriel summarized. "There is direct and clear; muted yet cumulatively telling; and finally, the cry of desperation. The first is the easiest. For the second, you need a good and attentive ear. It is the third kind that demands the most patience - but when they finally let go, you will know it."

"And, of course, there is the fourth group – the largest one – consisting of all the people we never hear from. Unfortunately, they are the kind of people we often hear *of* much later on."

Muted But Cumulative

"Got it," said Antonio, shaking his head. "Our training obviously is not over."

"Now all we have to do is *do* it," said Sarah with a big grin.

"All you really have to do," said Gabriel softly, "is listen with greater sensitivity – which is what we also advise humans to do with each other. Watch the body language. Listen for the nuances. Become acutely attuned to how humans express their needs, their pains, their longings, their loneliness. Don't wait for neon lettering on a billboard, a shout from the hilltops, or for a Soul to develop a highly noticeable physical disability or mental dysfunction."

"'I am lonely' - is a request," Gabriel explained. "'I need a hug' – is a request. 'I feel down and out' – is a way of asking for help. And when these kinds of sentiments accumulate, they amount to cries for help."

"And you always have the option - according to how dire things become and how empathetic you feel – of getting involved indirectly. You could, for example, always arrange for a so-called 'coincidence', a nudge, a very soft intervention that gives them some encouragement and some sense of support. Got it?" asked Gabriel.

"Oh my goodness, I never realized. Here we've been waiting for something dramatic, super obvious - that would shake our cloud with a seismic irruption," said Sarah.

Antonio agreed: "Yeah. If a call was not loud and clear, we tended to ignore it. Apparently, many have been asking – in many different ways - but we were not sensitive to the nuanced ways in which suffering and need – and thus a request - is expressed."

"It would be like my finally waiting for you to turn in your GAIT badges before offering you some assistance," said Gabriel, "when all I needed to do was tune into your long and loud litanies of disappointment, which I heard as an indirect but real request - and here I am!"

A Few More Words About 'Nudging'

"One more word – or two – if you will permit me," said Gabriel, "on this subject of nudging. As noted, when in doubt interact with your charges. Enter into their dream sequences, take a bodily form now and again and support them in some demonstrable way - like surrounding them with love as they go about the day. You can also enter into their mind sets as inspirations and surges of interest and motivation."

"You could even poke them with hints and subtle invitations, encounter them in so-called chance meetings and with subtle whispers, urge them to trust their own intuitions and hunches. Archangel Raphael is an absolute pro at this kind of stuff. Watch for him. Call on him. Follow his example. There is no spiritual force that is finer, more talented or more delightful to be with - then Raphael."

"And last, encourage your charges to shout out if their need is immediate or overwhelming in size and scope. If so, Archangel Michael will be at their – or your - side immediately. And his invention is known to be quite commanding and persuasive."

"In conclusion...and I now do mean to conclude," said Gabriel with a flourish - puffing his wings, revving up the intensity of his energy field, smiling at himself and then laughing out loud with his two angelic students:

"Sit on your cloud if you get tired, but never before that. This loving and counseling stuff involves a sacred partnership. So use your spiritual empowerments to act on what you sense and intuit as well as what you hear and see overtly. Expand your sensitivities and be a bit more proactive. If you allow the needs of your charges to reach your hearts as well as you ears – you'll never be under-employed again."

Dagney's Life Training

Dagney certainly was aware of her spiritual identity. But on an average day it was easily out-competed by life's general and cumulative busyness.

As a divorced mother of two, she was often too busy and too tired even to meditate for a few minutes no less nourish her conviction that she had incarnated on Earth many, many times before. She had memories of talking directly with God as a child and having recalls into her early adulthood of a set of earlier lifetimes. Although those connections had now faded from being numerous and vivid to occasional and vague, she never stopped thinking of herself as an immortal Soul, something like a tiny cell that was an integral part of a cosmic and divine being.

Despite her spiritual convictions, Sarah wisely did not quit her day job as a waitress in a high-end deli in New York City. She had three very physical mouths to feed and a monthly rent to pay. On the plus - and the minus - side, she also had a part time boyfriend who she both loved but also wanted to shed. Her road was not arduous but it was not paved with gold either.

Up at 5:30 a.m., out the door with the kids by 7:00, to work by 7:30 – an eight-hour shift at the deli got her home in time to insure the children did their homework. The contents of various boxes and cans

were then mixed creatively for the night's dinner. After a little TV, the usual hassles over baths, ten minutes of alone time with each child, and after few phone calls and reading a magazine article, the daily routine of her current incarnation came to a sleepy end.

The weekends mostly were fun — except when the boys and the boyfriend each vied for her exclusive attention. The kids were hers forever — 'they are the center of my life', she would say. "Jack: who knows? We have been dating for three years and he never has a dime to spend on me - or the children. And he's never willing to tell me where he thinks this relationship is going. Between my job and Jack - I know I definitely need my job."

Dreamtime is Travel Time

The hours between ten in the evening and five-thirty the next morning were often spent in a very different way. Dagney does not remember it all — all of the time — but she definitely wakes a few mornings a month with the sense that she has been traveling. That is, she has the distinct feeling that her Soul, freed from her body during the sleeping hours, wanders into the ether and participates in an entirely different universe.

So where the cliental at the deli is mostly male, white and Jewish, in the dream state she serves mostly black Muslim women and children. And while the fare during the day features a high-energy exchange of soups, sandwiches and salads, the evenings prompt only memories of low moans, bandages and small food parcels stamped with the insignia of the UN.

The work during the day is, of course, long and hard - so by evening she is understandably tired. And on most mornings she is still groggy. But whenever she awakes with recollections of travel and service, she feels restored, alert, re-energized — despite memories of lifting and turning wounded bodies, hauling beds and setting up tents as strong winds churned around her.

It is then that she knows her Soul has been to Haiti following its recent earthquake, or Darfur, the devastated area of western Sudan with

its millions of refugees. Frequently she wakes up in the morning with her thumb incessantly pushing down on her index finger – as if replicating an injection or a syringe.

And if the work at the deli - during the day - invariably includes laughter and warm friendship, it is her night travels and its labors that produce the greatest sense of love and satisfaction. Yet the joy and encouragement she receives during the day from co-workers – and even customers – seems to create that extra reservoir of energy she needs during those nights when the dreams are the most intense, when she often feels overwhelmed by the magnitude of suffering and the sheer horror of the refugee camps.

Yet just as she finds herself ready to scream in desperation, she senses a flutter - like a soft but pronounced breath of scented air - and a woman by the name of Sarah suddenly arrives, smiling, picking up on the conversation they had minutes - or was it weeks ago? Again, and again – it is Sarah: super energetic, doing the work of ten attendants, lifting spirits, curing others through her actions and healing them with her presence.

"How did you know I – we - needed help?" Dagney would ask.

"I heard you," answered Sarah.

"How did you get here?"

"The same way - you did."

"Who are you – really?"

"I am the same as you – only I transit *from* the other side while you transit *to* your other side."

Introducing James

James always wakes up with a headache. It could be the incessant smoking, the evening six-pack, the poor diet – or all three, a combination

reflecting a fitful life filled with more starts than finishes. Three jobs ago, two apartments ago, and "that girlfriend – Louie's niece – the one before Janet, who lived in Queens somewhere, oh gawd – I can never remember her name" – is the best way to describe his life.

Wish I could turn my life around, he thought to himself as he shaved. I have been praying of late - but I don't even know what to ask for except for some clarity in my life and the ability to contribute to something larger than my own selfish interests. Then there are all those crying jags – like, out of nowhere – when I'm mush - sprawled out on the couch, wasted.

Joey, my cousin, knows a lot about spiritual stuff. He is not a religious guy, per se, but he puts everything into the perspective by literally 'trusting everything'. "You create your universe so you need to trust whatever you attract," says he. He is also inclined to love everybody and empathize with everything – which is a little much – but he's a good guy. So he suggests that I meditate, just sit still for like ten minutes, which I try but without much success.

Then there's his wildest suggestion - that I contact my Guardian Angel. But what do I know about such things? In my own way, I try, I ask – but nothing has happened. Who knows?

James flips to the back of the paper – where all the so-called practical stuff is: personals, funny ads, the sexual fantasy come-ons, and of course the list of sales: 'Headboard & Qn Mattress (Brand New), Only $100', or 'Chest-o-Drawers, Mediterranean, Spec Today, $85', and the ever present, 'Going Out of Business: Jewelry, Gold Brac, Pearl Nklcs: Jerry's, Third & Union. This Ad =$25'. And, of course, there is the daily horoscope.

"More coffee, hon?" asks the waitress.

"Yeah, of course, thanks. And today, Laura, I'm starting a new approach to life: something about Uranus transiting Saturn, you know the symbol of change colliding with the symbol of stability and - boom,

there's change, maybe even a revolution, and for the better. It's all here in the paper."

"Yeah?" says Laura, looking over the top of her glasses.

"Sounds good, eh?" says James thumping his index finger on the paper. "If you don't mind, today I am gonna have two eggs, over light – if you don't mind – but no sausage, noooo sausage," says James. "As of this minute, I am starting to take good care of myself – inside and out, if you know what I mean. And orange juice, yeah – a large OJ. And plain whole wheat toast… no butter… dry… okay?!"

"If you say so," says Laura. "It's gonna upset the cosmic balance in the kitchen – but I'll place the order… and we'll see what happens."

"Hey guys," she yells, as she pushes inside the swinging door, "waita ya hear this."

Heeding the Call

It was a Saturday and the weather was lovely, so James, in his new zeal for all things healthy, decided to walk. And walk he did, first through the area of small ethnic food shops – where he picked up a small fruit-cake (his compromise for the day) and a bottle of water. He then sipped and munched as he passed the theater, inspected a line of sidewalk art, and browsed through several boxes of used books – all of which took him to the edge of the park … with its monastery up high on the hill.

For some reason, the bells were chiming in the campanile. It was only one o'clock. "Must be a wedding," thought James. "Good for them – whoever they are. Somebody's got to get it right – at least once in a while. Think I'll go and see. Maybe sit in the back. At least it will be good to watch other people celebrate. And who knows, some times church music can be worth listening to – especially if there's a chorus."

James could not remember ever having been to this particular monastery or its main church. It was always 'that place on the hill' that he

viewed in the distance - although seeing it usually generated a vague memory of having walked down its corridors many times before.

I can almost hear the footsteps echoing in the marble hallways, he said to himself. Well, today's my day. The bell tower, a wedding — maybe even the cloisters will be open. Might at well go and take a look. Strike one for Uranus!

He crossed the traffic circle, walked around the small pond, and then started up the gradual incline that swung in a half circle along a thick stand of trees. The black asphalt was quiet - but not the crushed stone; its crackling sound momentarily startled James as he stepped onto the path leading to the large embroidered gate. The church was to the left, the campanile in the middle, and a cascade of gothic buildings – which he assumed was the monastery - were on the right.

He stopped in front of the church, looked at the bell tower rising six stories into what was then a pure blue sky — and suddenly realized the obvious. There was no one else around. The bells were quiet. There was no wedding or any other service in progress. Aside from the sound of his footsteps, all was silent. He was the only one in the courtyard.

Strange. So now, what do I do? The doors to the Church appear to be open. Maybe somebody is in there. Might as well give it a try. He climbed the three stone steps, passed through the large oak doors, walked into the vestibule, gently pushed against the swinging doors, and entered the Church.

The vaulting must have reached sixty feet high. Tall stained glass windows extended all the way up the nave - each framed in dark wood. Double rows of smaller windows also lined the wings or side aisles. Colored light flooded the chamber. 'Wow,' was all James remembers saying as he retold the story later on. He slowly advanced up the main aisle – hushed by the grandeur of the silence and the lush surroundings. He paused, then stopped - halfway to the altar – entered a row of pews, lifted the kneeler with his shoe, sat back … and exhaled.

Silence. Nothing but silence.

Silence, Colors and Then – a Monk

James sat for the longest time, at first leaning forward on the row of seats in front of him, then sitting back again to admire the full scope of the setting.

What am I doing here, he said to himself, as he stroked his forehead. Uranus and new starts, eh? I have been lost. How *do* I get found? I sure don't want to continue doing what I have been doing now for years. I want to make a new start. But how? Oh, God – he prayed in silence: I really do need some help!

The prolonged silence continued, that is, until James heard the soft ringing of the church bells – the same bells, he concluded that had beckoned to him when he stood at the bottom of the hill. After climbing the hill, he anticipated finding ceremony and being a bystander to a marriage celebration. Now the church was empty and this second ringing of the bells seemed to invite him to just listen. Gazing up and all around him, he was again dazzled by the harmony of color and sound. Everything seems to reverberate – even the candles along the altar flickered with an extra exuberance. If he was going to be renewed, he thought, this is a wonderful way to start.

Suddenly, he heard a door swing open, then close. The sound came from a darkened area just to the left of the altar. Footsteps, faint at first, became increasingly clear and distinct as they grew near. A tall figure was walking straight toward him – dressed in a dark brown robe, white rope at his waist, his monk's cowl pulled up and around his face.

The monk stopped and bowed his head slightly, the outline of his face emerging gradually as he bent closer. He was smiling and both hands were extended. "Come, James," it said with a gentle but cheerful whisper. "Let's wander around - even visit the courtyards and the

inner rooms of the cloister. If you want, you might even get to ring the bells - again — as you did many years ago."

The Marble Hallways

James followed the hooded figure — as if in a daze. All of this was wild, crazy, surreal - he concluded — starting with the newspaper and breakfast, the walk, the bells, the empty silence of the monastery. Now a hooded figure — I assume a monk who lives here — invites me to tour the place. If I already had a life, I certainly would not be here. So who am I to refuse?

The hallways were darkened except for the natural light that shone through the upper transoms. And as they walked, James was both fascinated and puzzled. "I do not remember ever being in this exact monastery before. But I do have a strong feeling of having been in hallways like this before — when I was once a knight, or a monk, or a religious warrior of some sort."

He felt the wall, examined the floor and glanced up at the ceiling. They were all made of stone - and now resonated to every footstep like an echo chamber.

"Now I absolutely know I have walked and hurried through such hallways many times before - sometimes during periods of great commotion," he said to the monk walking beside him. "Exactly where and when exactly, I can't remember. But I know the resonating sound of this stone - like I know the sound of the bells."

"Well," said the monk, "you are absolutely right when you say you have been in such hallways before."

"When?"

"Oh — during several lifetimes around 1120 to 1314 when you were a member of the Knights Templar in Malta."

"In fact," the monk continued, "you – as a Soul in other incarnations – have spent many a lifetime in the direct service of several spiritual traditions: as a priest, a minister, a warrior knight, a monk in Anglo-Saxon England and even a Buddhist monk-gardener (in both India and Japan). This may also help to explain why you are so fascinated by my robes. You have worn similar outfits – many, many times before."

"You are kidding me, aren't you"? said James.

"No, not at all," laughed the monk. "Come let's walk in the inner gardens. Just relax and enjoy what you see. You may not recall all the details – which is fine. Slowly but surely, however, you will remember enough to realize that you have indeed been various people during your many previous incarnations – and many of them were spiritual in nature."

"In fact," said the monk, "you may even recall why you choose the themes of your current life and your present style of living."

"As a punishment or some kind of karma, I assume," said James.

No Punishment

"No," smiled the monk. "There really is no such thing as punishment or karma that necessarily carries over from one lifetime to another. Souls often do choose to revisit a situation if they feel they did not handle it well in an earlier life, or a certain difficulty in order to learn a lesson they avoided earlier. But most selections – however great the challenge – have a positive twist: to increase a Soul's ability to love thus add to their spiritual depth and psychological wholeness."

"So this time," he continued, "you deliberately chose to learn - first hand - what it is like to lose your way, to live a life that up until now has lacked much love or made much of a contribution or included the sense of being close to God. But you started to change all that – and

reclaim your spiritual core - a few weeks ago when you asked for help in dealing with your difficulties."

"I repeat: the challenges you have faced until now are the same ones you chose to experience before you entered into your current incarnation," the monk continued. "You – like every other Soul - designed the basic framework of your earthly life before you re-incarnated - including the outline of what is happening today."

"Wow', and I mean 'wow'," said James. "Each one of your comments are like revelations - which although they seem wild and impossible – they also ring true. So I feel overwhelmed by what you are saying, and want to resist it. Yet – simultaneously – I feeling uplifted by your comments and literally invited to finally 'wake up'. It's like a struggle between the old traditional me who has just been bumping around through life, and the new – or maybe 'the really old' - Soul in me that honors everything you say and wants definitely to follow its lead."

"What is particularly wonderful," said the monk, "is that this is the time you decided to be both overwhelmed and awakened. Look at the cumulative buildup. It all started weeks ago when you began praying for guidance. And today there has been one symbolic invitation and breakthrough after another: the shift you associated with the horoscope and the energy of Uranus, your sudden and instinctual decision to revolutionize what you eat for breakfast, your desire to change your string of debilitating habits, your intuitive opening to a more meaningful commitment – all of it helping you, finally – to notice the monastery, hear the bells and propel you up the hill."

"Given all your hard work and your growing receptivity to your own inner Soulfulness, I could not resist ringing the bells of the campanile," smiled the monk. "It signaled your 'tipping point', so the speak, enticing you to the church and then into the sanctuary where you emphatically asked for help. Coming up the hill was a critical turning point which you consolidated once you were in the chapel."

"You?" said James in amazement.

"Yes?" answered the monk – nodding his head.

"Gawd. I am stunned. Once I entered the church, I did pray a few times, yes. And a friend advised me – in time of need - to call on God or at least what he called my 'Guardian Angel.' So I also thought about that and I guess I did ask God and my Guardian Angel for help."

"Well, you were smart enough to invoke the most basic of divine laws: 'Ask, and it will be given to you, search and you will find; knock and the door will be opened to you' - to quote one of your sacred books, Matthew 7: 7, I believe."

"And you are part of that response?"

"Yup!"

"And, with all due respect, please - tell me: who are you?"

"Ahhhhhhh, I, my beloved friend: I am – Antonio – your Guardian Angel, here at your service."

Not One or the Other: Both!

James and Antonio then walked through the maze of courtyards, and then slowly made their way back into the chapel. They walked slowly, side by side, saying not a word, just traversing the grounds like two old friends.

They re-entered the church at a side door, and returned to the row and the seat that James occupied earlier. He sat down, and soon began to weep, first covering his eyes and then his entire face, slumping forward, overwhelmed by all he had experienced.

"First a large OJ, then a walk up the hill, and now my Guardian Angel - speaking to me in person – no less," said James out loud. "Antonio: it's amazing, and all in the same day," he muttered, laughing through his tears.

Apparently everything was related: the newspaper story, the meandering walk, sighting the Church, the chimes of the bell tower, the empty Church, then the appearance of a monk who turns out to be his Guardian Angel! Was it all a series of coincidences - a string of random happenings - or an orchestrated and willed set of breakthroughs? Perhaps, he thought to himself: could it be that 'this is normal', this is what happens — 'all the time' - in the spiritual world? Amazing, absolutely amazing.

He looked up in time to see the robed figure disappearing down the side aisle. Nearing the doorway, Antonio paused to interact with what appeared to be an elderly woman. Her left hand was resting on the altar rail, while her right arm was lifted — and pointing to the center aisle.

James looked as well, and as he did, another woman - seated next to him - suddenly turned and gently tapped his arm.

"Doesn't she look beautiful," she said as they both looked to the altar. A young couple, smiling, had just turned to accept the cheers of family and friends. The bride held the groom's arm, and they proceeded down the few steps leading to the main aisle. People were clapping and cheering, and some were even shouting out their blessings.

"It's all so grand," said the woman, "I have known the groom since he was this high. Used to deliver my newspapers. Oh lord save us: what a wonderful day. And now listen to those bells. There is indeed much to celebrate."

James was transfixed. The experience with the monk - with Antonio — had actually happened, he exclaimed to himself. We walked. We talked. We shared. He was here. And all the silence: when I arrived, when I entered the Church, when I sat here alone and prayed - as I noticed and was then invited by Antonio to see the inner space of the monastery.

I know I experienced it all, he kept saying to himself. Yet apparently, all *this* - the marriage ceremony - was happening simultaneously: hundreds of people had congregated, wandered in, chatted, took their places, witnessed and participated in another sacred ritual, all of it – all of it - unfolding at the same time.

Oh - my – gawd, was the only thing he remembered mumbling. Slow down. Think this through, he said to himself. My experience with Antonio was real. Yet this world – this woman, the smiling couple, the crowd - are all real too. The bells! They rang as I started my transit up the hill. Antonio rang them again once I literally prayed and asked for help. And they are ringing again now as I reenter this material world and scene of the wedding ceremony.

Where is the veil that separates one realm from the other? And what is it that activates the passage from one to the other? Is it in us, in the way our consciousness happens to operate? Does prayer really help? Incredible. If so, how do I live in and integrate both realms? How do I – or anyone – combine one with the other, guide one with the other, live in both worlds, choose to be a spiritual being who lives and operates in a material universe?

Must walk – again – clear my head – maybe find a quiet spot and pray...or meditate... just get some fresh air.

So James instinctively reached back to retrieve his half full bottle of water and the remnants of his Italian fruitcake.

He felt for the bottle. Yes.

As to the paper bag: it was there as well.

But what is this – a third item?

His hand clutched a rope. It was a white rope. It had been folded in half and apparently twirled, the two parts entwined like a caduceus – with the ends tied loosely in a knot.

Enter – An Archangel

"Nice job."

"I am sorry I cannot hear you," yelled Antonio to the huge field of energy vibrating immediately in front of him.

"Sorry. Sometimes I forget to calm down my vibrations. There: can you hear me now?"

"Yes – your voice and features are beginning to come through clearly," said Antonio. "Initially the rush of energy scared me: it was as loud and pulsating as a hundred hands clapping or a million bees buzzing – if I can use such earthly metaphors."

The visitor laughed. "How's this?" he asked.

"Yes – now – it's fine. Thank you," said Antonio.

"I just wanted to congratulate you. You did some lovely work with James."

"Is that you, Raphael? Oh my goodness. Gabriel mentioned you as a potential resource, but I never expected to see you so soon."

"Well here I am – unexpected as usual," laughed Raphael. "I just happen along whenever it seems right. May I float along with you?" he asked.

"But of course," said Antonio immediately as he looked up at the glowing field of energy that was now at his side.

"Ah: the white rope. A great touch. Good thinking," Raphael stressed. "James needed that, something to verify his experience. All day he experienced one mini awakening after another: it was a lot to absorb. And don't worry: he won't sell the rope, and he is smart enough not to worship it, although he may mention it one day in confidence to one of his most trusted – and I might add – beloved colleagues."

"I do sense he will heed its healing symbolism, however," Raphael added, "and even follow its lead as he seeks answers to his questions. Otherwise, it will stay in the drawer with his best tee-shirts and New York Yankee memorabilia."

"Thank you, Raphael. To tell you the truth I was hesitant at first. This was my first big case," said Antonio. "Just going through the Akashic Records in search of James' previous incarnations was in itself an incredible experience. It was my first time to work with the archives of the universe. I just keyed in on anything to do with marble floors, Knights, monasteries and bells - and all the cross-references and identities fell into place."

"It was a very, very humbling and wondrous," Antonio concluded. "I never dreamed of receiving God's permission to research an immortal Soul's history. Frankly, I am still shaking and teary-eyed. The honor of being that close to Prime Source is something I will never forget."

"Well, let's use the experience to extend both *your* training as a Guardian Angel, and *James'* awakening interest in his spiritual identity," said Raphael. "I'm delighted to be of assistance. Shall we flow with the wind currents? I always love seeing the variety of flora and fauna with which Earth is blessed."

"I am delighted to follow your lead," said Antonio. "And if you don't mind my saying so, it is a great honor to be in your company. This is turning out to be as wild and wonderful for me as it apparently is for James."

Raphael

"De nada," said Raphael, known for his friendly and informal ways. His name means "God has healed" as well as "the shining one who heals". In Earthly art he is associated with the healing image of serpents and the caduceus, and is usually depicted as a merry and witty companion who simply arrives unannounced — and coincidentally, if you are willing — to

be of assistance to one and all, especially the average person. He is also one of the seven Angels of the Apocalypse. His healing capacities are mentioned in 1 Enoch and several Kabalistic and Gnostic legends. They are also described in the Book of Tobias – as depicted in a 1470 painting by Verrocchio .

"Forgive me," says Antonio," but I could not notice your six wings – which seem to be ablaze, indicating you are also a Seraph, one of the 'burning ones' inflamed by God's love and understanding."

"Ah – be gone with you," said Raphael laughing. "No Seraphim, Dominion, Archangel – or any of the other angelic powers - are any better than a 'Guardian Angel in Training'. And no worst either!" he chuckled. "Every aspect of the entire spiritual hierarchy – including the billions of human Souls – have their mandates and missions, and we all blend together in the service of Prime Source."

"So we are all involved in a sacred partnership," Raphael emphasized, "aiding and assisting whoever we can, whenever we can. But the primary focus of our little partnership – in this situation and at *this* eternal moment – is the triad of you, Me and our friend James."

"I'm all for it," said Antonio, stepping back a pace and raising his head so he could look Raphael in the eye. "Zow," was all he could say next, followed by "Amazing. Simply Amazing."

Working With James

"That's the spirit… pun intended," responded Raphael - as his energy field again glowed and puffed from his laughter.

"Might I suggest two ways of dealing with James," he continued. "The first deals with the kind of energy he seems to need most, namely *enlightenment*. It will effect how he operates and then will help him convert his recent breakthroughs into spiritual realities."

"Ah – be gone with you," said Raphael laughing. "No Seraphim, Domin-ion, Archangel – or any of the other angelic powers - are any better than a 'Guardian Angel in Training'. And no worst either!" he chuckled.

"The second concerns his focus, namely what he chooses to do with that enlightened energy. In James's case, he may not be aware of it yet, but I sense he possesses great potential as a teacher and as an agent of healing. Put the two together and that points to James teaching others how to convey healing energies to those in need."

"Thus the fit," said Raphael. "Both themes – *enlightenment* and *heal-ing* – are among my primary empowerments – which is probably why

Prime Source assigned me to this case. And you would not be here - working with James as his Guardian Angel- unless God was also asking you to enhance your enlightening and healing energies too. You may still be in training but obviously Prime Source is already expressing confidence in bolstering your repertoire."

"I'm honored," said Antonio.

"God does not give out medals or commendations when She's pleased. Rewards tend to come in the form of greater responsibility. So be careful you don't get really good at this Guardian Angelic stuff – or the workload will get mighty heavy and fast," said Raphael, grinning and lightly flapping two of his six wings at his side.

Enlightenment

"Now," said Raphael, "let's look more closely at each arena. First, the energy of *enlightenment*."

"There are two different approaches to enlightenment. Many – throughout the human millennia – have treated it a something to be attained only after serious and hard work. We call them the 'chapped lips brigade'. Invite the challenge, nose to the grindstone, suffer as you travel a long and disciplined road – all that kind of stuff – and eventually a person earns their stripes and comes to see the universe from a spiritual point of view."

"Well that route works for those who have the will and talent to make it work, and work it is. If that's what they like, more power to them. But others, like me, tend to see enlightenment not so much as something accomplished after an arduous routine but more as a joyful and appreciative affirmation of what is already at hand. The key to this route to enlightenment is literally to 'lighten up'!"

"It is like the stroll we are now taking," said Raphael with a twinkle in his eye. "It need not involve furrowed browses, white knuckles, burning coals, gallons of midnight oil, long hours on your knees or sequestered away like a mole in the library. Rather, enlightenment can

be activated by the immediate acceptance – and thus experience - of God's love and joy and the absolute beauty of our universe. Enlightenment from this perspective – already is. It approaches everything as a gift, as an opportunity to lighten up and appreciate life, to embrace it and its constant invitation *now*, to be loving and joyful beginning right *now*. Bing-badda-bing, badda-boom."

Now that set Raphael off on a round of snickers, chuckles and outright belly laughter, so much so that Antonio could not help but join in.

"Of my," Raphael resumed. "That felt good."

"Now where were we?" he said to himself.

"This second route to enlightenment," said Antonio, still regaining his composure.

"Ah, yes, yes, of course," chortled Raphael.

"If we take the 'lighter' way – which I sense we will," said Antonio with a grin, "then how does it apply to James – and I – if we are to work together effectively?"

"Well," snickered Raphael, "get rid of the serious resolve 'to work together – effectively'," he said with a deep falsetto voice and grave inflection. "Remember Gandhi's lifestyle: 'Be what you wish to create.'"

"There's no need to be serious and concerned with how you can best serve James. You are an empowered, loving and joyful being. Just be who you already are. James will love it - because, he too, wants to unfold, he too wants to stop suffering and complaining, he too wants to trust his capacity to serve and live - fully - now," said Raphael with a gentle smile.

Inner And Outer Radiance

Antonio was quiet for the longest time, kept nodding his head, then wiped his eyes.

"Oh, I apologize for the glare," Raphael said, as he deliberately toned down the colors of his radiance. "When I get excited, all of me tends to gets excited!"

"Now I don't mean to put outer radiance down," he commented. "No way. Being enlightened includes the capacity to spread 'the light', to so radiate with inner love and joy that it is naturally expressed outwardly. These are the folks that tend to 'glow' no matter what they are doing or where they are."

"As to my extra glare," he added, "I think it comes from being depicted this way throughout the history of western art. It's apparently the result of a reverse bleed through. Basically, I see myself as just an average angel — with a little extra coloring! It's silly- but I have learned to live with it," he said impishly. "Besides"- nudging Antonio in his left wing - "Archangels have egos too." And he laughed again — this time with such gusto that the surrounding clouds bounced up and down, then turned blue, then green, then bright red.

"Where were we?" he asked. "Ah, yes: when you 'lighten up' and honor it for what it is — an incredible gift of God — then your enlightened attitude is naturally reflected in your words, demeanor and actions — even under somber circumstances. In short, you, and James, and I, and all of us - have the capacity to create light whenever we are light."

"Got it?"

"Yes - I think so," said Antonio.

Then he quickly corrected himself: "Please make that an emphatic and joyful 'yes — I got it!'" he said with emphasis and clarity — and then a big smile.

"Bingo. Fantastico," responded Raphael.

"Now, one more thing: if you ever get stuck or confused, find a reason to laugh first…even if it is at yourself. If you need prompting, then you could even recall one of your foibles or something you said or did that was really silly. When your heart is awakened with laughter, it's impossible not to activate your lighter side."

"As to the other factor," Raphael continued, "namely James' awareness of his power to teach and heal: let's work with him directly and help him choose exactly how and when he wishes to express his potential. Given what happened today, I'd be surprised if he wasn't already aware of his hidden talents."

Healing

James looked at his hands. They were tingling – then soon felt like they were both drawing in energy, and alternatively emitting it. Strange, he thought. My hands are good indicators of how I feel - but they've never felt quite like this before. I'm half way down the hill from the monastery. Best stop for a moment, sit here on this park bench, think things through.

As James prayed for guidance on what to do with everything that had happened that day, his attention kept returning to his hands. They did not sweat or hurt, but they did feel more vibrant and alive than ever. Obviously they were not separate from his arm or his body but they did feel strangely distinct.

He had never worked predominantly with his hands – as do farmers and ranchers, artists and tradesmen. He had worked in an office for many years – organizing the flow of people, money and goods. But none of his several jobs involved anything that fully engaged his mind, his hands or any other part of his body. That in fact was the cause of his boredom, his poor attitude and resultant dismissals. He did use his hands a lot for drawing when young - mostly cartoons. And he

always wanted to learn how to play a musical instrument but never did.

As long as he could remember, however, his hands were a means to clarify how he felt about a situation. They were also his barometers for gauging the truth-value of what was happening at a given moment; their feedback was nearly always immediate and well near infallible.

Dryness, for example, was usually a sign of being tired. But a really deep sense of ease and calm indicated he was at peace with himself. Itchy hands were the sign of boredom, and an agitated feeling usually indicated he needed something about which he was either unaware or not yet acted on. Very soft and moist palms suggested he was out of balance or nervous while cool moisture along his fingers was a sure sign of excitement and participation.

Full-bloodedness indicated the advent of something new and exciting. But this feeling of drawing in and sending out energy was new, and that is how his hands had been feeling since he left the church.

"Ah, a clue – and an opening," Antonio said to Raphael as – unbeknownst to James – the two of them hovered near the end of the bench on which James was sitting.

"And what do you hear of his internal dialogue?" asked the smiling Archangel.

"He is feeling energetic," said Antonio.

"What kind of energy?'

"Pulsating, full, flowing, alive."

"What does it tell you?"

"He needs, no – wants – to act, to go forward."

"To what end?"

"He has an inkling it involves something spiritual - but is still unsure and thus a little hesitant."

"Telling you what?"

"He needs – and is very willing to accept - some nudging, some assistance – to help him clarify how he wants to contribute and where."

"And given recent experiences, what aspects of himself is he wanting to develop?"

"Why his spiritual identity, of course."

"And which aspect of himself is most likely to trust – and use?"

"His hands. He trusts them to verify how he feels and what he senses. Now he is becoming aware of how they can receive and send energy. I've noticed in the past that when he's faced with toxic people or situations, for example, he tends to close his hands and fold them into his body. In healthy or positive situations, his hands tend to be out, open and up."

"To the top of the class with you," howled Raphael. "Spiritual energy when conveyed through the hands, with the intention of helping another, is one of the most powerful ways of transmitting *healing energy!*"

"And James is now a prime candidate for such empowerments. He is changing his lifestyle and consciously embracing his spiritual core, physical and psychological conditions that make for an excellent healing medium. It appears he is fast becoming the full and real-deal."

"Now to arrange for a more specific calling or annunciation," said Raphael, "a sort of tipping point that will activate his potential. And you, my dear Antonio, are exactly the right Guardian Angel - in exactly the right spot - to spur him on its way."

So it was that Gabriel and Antonio arranged for an ad to appear in the newspaper that James still loved to peruse every morning at the

diner – the same one that had intrigued him earlier with its announcement of the Uranus-Saturn transit and its symbolism of revolutionary change.

Sending and Receiving Healing Energy

The announcement read: "An Inter-Denominational Meeting. Saturday evening at 8. Featuring Robert Realto, Healing Medium, in a lecture-demonstration on *'How to Invoke and Transfer Healing Energies.'*"

Only ten people attended. There was a middle aged man and woman, the female minister of the church, two teen-agers, an elderly couple, a reporter from the local newspaper, James, and of course, Robert (a.k.a. GAIT Antonio). The group gathered on the ground floor of the Church on the hill.

Robert greeted the group, and immediately explained that healing was evident in every historical civilization because it was a universally inspired way of helping others - emotionally and physically. It involved three factors: divinely inspired healing energy; a medium who received, then transferred the energy; and a recipient who choose to receive the energy for a healing purpose.

Robert emphasized that the recipient was, in essence, their own healer – because they assented to the transfer and were free to use it as they saw fit: clear their mind of fear and anxiety, help with an emotional issue, open themselves to a spiritual mission, help with a physical difficulty or aid in the development of a desired character trait (such as patience, creativity, empathy or whatever).

The medium is the so-called middleman who with a pure heart invokes God's healing energy and serves as a clear and loving channel who transmits the energy to the recipient.

"It is a simple process when the medium and recipient are aligned, but a very complicated - if not impossible - one when they are not,"

said Robert. "So it helps for everyone to approach it with a light heart. So it is best to relax, to be at ease, and trust in God. Do not try to make it happen. Simply allow it to unfold. Healing is a way of celebrating God's creativity."

Robert led the group in asking for God's guidance and support, and they formed teams of two, one person volunteering to receive the energy and the other invoking and conveying it. When finished, they switched roles.

"Remember," said Robert, "this is a process of giving and receiving. So approach it with loving intention - and all will be well and wondrous. You are meant to benefit from it. So relax – enter into it with confidence and a sense of light-heartedness. It is serious, of course, but you are also meant to enjoy yourselves."

He looked over to where he knew Raphael was hovering – and smiled. He then heard those magic words – this time in the form of a whisper: "Bingo! Fantastico."

James Steps Up

The comments made throughout the evening were revealing.

"I've been sending loving energies to friends and family – even passersby – for years but never knew what to call it. 'Healing' sounds too biblical for an average person like me."

"I loved both giving and receiving . I didn't know what I was doing but I really enjoyed it."

"The energy I felt coming from that young man's hands was amazing. It was like getting a double dose of caffeine while being surrounded by a heating pad."

"Yeah, I loved everything – but especially want to work with you – yes: you, young man – if there is a next time."

"I never trusted my hands to do much but clean house. This was so much more enjoyable. And my back, oh my aching back, feels better already. When's the next session?"

"Everyone was so nice, so open, so willing, and so gracious. Can I take you all home!"

"It was really nice to have someone thank me for sending them energy. I like doing that. And it was so good to be attended to by so many loving people."

It was 10:45 before the group expressed a strong desire to meet again the following week. Robert agreed to return — and did so for the next three weeks - by which time people were routinely arriving early and staying late.

James was popular, was obviously in his element, and was now in demand. Many wanted to partner with him or at least observe him in the healing role. So he found himself counseling others - before and after each partnership was formed.

"There is no one way," he would say when asked about his breathing, mindset and placement of his hands. "Just trust yourself, focus on a loving image, pretend you're a floor lamp and you're here to spread your kind of light in your naturally loving way."

Several people had difficulty concentrating and centering themselves, so James also started a mini class on 'how to meditate' - a half hour before the main meeting.

"Love it, love it, love it. It is helping me to be me - not just for healing - but for everything," said an accountant who wore a suit to the first meeting but jeans and a tee-shirt ever since.

The enthusiasm of the original group naturally attracted friends and even a few family members. In the meantime, an article appeared in the newspaper, and soon the attendance averaged 25-30 people. It became

obvious that the group needed a coordinator. James was nominated, accepted and was elected unanimously.

"Best things I ever did was order orange juice, walk up that hill, and join this group," he would admit to anyone who asked. And that was not just a commentary on his spiritual life. As you will soon find out, that transition set the stage for similar changes in his personal life, his professional life and – you guessed it – his romantic life as well.

Sacred Conversation

The area was hushed – as it usually is just before the Archangels meet. Only this occasion was extra-special. Prime Source had especially asked to chat with Gabriel and Raphael.

Then a third figure was asked to attend. He was tall, young, resplendent in a bejeweled coat of arms, holding a long lance in one hand, his mighty sword sheathed at this side. It was Michael, the warrior, the protector, the slayer of the unjust - invited not only because of his ability to deter aggression and protect the innocent but because he was also a psycho-pomp, one of the Angels of death and transition who conducted Souls departing the material world back to their original home in the spiritual realm.

Prime Source called the meeting in order to obtain a progress report on certain spiritual initiatives.

One: the program for the training of new Guardian Angels.

Two: the capacity of human Souls to serve as out-of-body spirits when their physical bodies were asleep.

And three: the ability of human incarnates to activate and convey healing to one another.

God's Priorities

"And as of this meeting," said God (also known as Prime Source), "in order to guarantee greater protection for all those involved in these

initiatives, I am hereby requesting that Archangel Michael spread his wings, so to speak, over all three initiatives - protecting all the participants and teaching them to wield, as necessary, a symbolic replica of his mighty sword."

"Now then, to the issues at hand," Prime Source continued. "As you know, the universe is expanding rapidly – not only the physical realities we know as galaxies, black holes and space itself – but in the number of Souls needed to populate and spiritualize these material realities."

"Our mission," Prime Source continued, "is to co-create an ever expansive and deepening Kosmos – as the Greeks on Earth rightly called it – namely, everything that is capable of being manifest as a reflection of our divinity: every thought and emotion, every aspect of every civilization, and every material thing that can be created by its inhabitants – including all the gadgets and tinker toys humans think are essential" - at which He paused to chuckle in sympathetic amusement.

"Then there are the space ships our Ascended Masters employ to monitor developments throughout the physical cosmos," said God. "And, of course, the all-encompassing nature of the Kosmos includes every piece of music, art and literature; every loving *and* self-satisfying word every uttered or printed by the various religious, philosophic, social and political organizations – the latter being well known for pushing it to its limits - and every scientific advance and engineering mechanism ever created – and to be created - by the many species that now inhabit the universe."

"It appears, however, that the creative capacities of our Kosmos could – at some juncture – expand faster than the physical universe itself. This will become a particular problem if the present focus on producing material goods - much of it silly and selfish - overwhelms the primacy of love among our inhabitants."

"In other words," Prime Source continued, "we need to stimulate the innate capacity of our creative Souls to be every mindful of their

immortal Souls and care for one another with increased empathy and compassion. Thus the initiatives to perfect and expand the training of Guardian Angels, the effort to encourage Souls to serve in their nightly 'out-of-body' travels, and our desire to stimulate humans to convey healing energies to one another."

Her conclusion: "The ability of Souls to create during their material incarnations, should, of course, continue. But we need to balance their ability to create ideas and things with an equal capacity, as Archangel Raphael puts it, 'to lighten up', to see themselves for who they are - immortal Souls here to create and contemplate a sacred universe. If so, they would then recognize and honor everything – *ev-er-y-thing* - as a reflection of a sacred universe. It might also quiet them once in a while – for prayer, for meditation and just to give thanks."

There was a long silence. The Archangels, as close to God as is possible, noticed that God's natural good cheer blurred ever so slightly – for but a nano-second. In that fraction of a moment, however, a deep sadness seemed to pervade the divine presence, and hint of moisture seemed to appear in Her eyes.

Quietude and solitude – the province of divinity – slowly faded, and as God finally looked up She gently brushed a cloud bank off her shoulder. The Archangels remained perfectly still. Then She spoke and with absolute clarity. Her voice was gentle, and Her words - uttered with great softness – yet were so poignant that they rumbled throughout the universe:

"The outer Kosmos does indeed appear to be flourishing," She admitted. "It is the inner one that needs deeper development. As always, We all have work to do."

Progress Reports

Gabriel then reported on the initiative with GAIT's Sarah and their work with the human incarnate called Dagney. Raphael then shared

the progress made in working with the Angel Antonio and his charge named James. And Michael outlined the ways in which he would both exercise his protective powers and bequeath the energy of his sword to anyone leading a spiritual initiative.

As the three Archangels were sharing particulars and getting advice from Prime Source, a messenger arrived with an urgent request. It was from Antonio. It seems an article appeared in the newspaper that included an accusation of 'witchery' among those who met 'in secret' each month at the hillside church. The rumor was picked up on the blogger-sphere, and an angry mob was now gathering outside the church.

"I'll go," said Raphael "the GAIT, Antonio is one of my charges."

"Really I should also go," said Gabriel, "since I am now working on a similar situation which will soon involve Sarah and Dagney."

"My dear colleagues: the outbreak of conflict and the need for protection really suggests that I also get to the scene immediately," asserted Michael.

"Haw," said Prime Source. "Please: each and all of you – like the Three Musketeers – off you go."

"Oh my," S/He laughed, as the three Archangels prepared to zoom their way to Earth. "How silly of that mob to provoke the three of you. They will not only be forced to back off by Michael, end up being encouraged by Gabriel to exercise their spiritual potential, and learn to both lighten up and facilitate healing others as they deal with Raphael. Be off, and God speed. We will continue when you return."

Michael's Mighty Sword

It was nearing the end of day and twilight was spreading rapidly. The incessant drizzle may have discouraged some but there were still 30-40 people assembled across the street from the Church. Some carried placards: "Witches Be Gone" read one, and "Burn Witches Burn"

was carried by an eight year old boy clutching the hand of a middle age man. It took two people to hold the ends of another sign filled with drawings of brooms, skeletons and poison bottles. Others shouted epithets. A threesome chanted, "Godless Get Out".

James and his colleagues had gathered an hour earlier, beginning with their normal 'meet and greet', a short meditation, and then sharing their 'progress reports'. There were stories of sending and receiving loving cards and e-mails, filling scrapbooks with pictures of people helping each other, sending spontaneous energy to people in passing, and, of course, reports of healing sessions conducted with family and friends.

Only then did the group break up into its now customary format: trios – with each person rotating between being the recipient of energy, the conveyer of it, and an observer who monitored the process and the subsequent de-briefing. It was this part of the meeting that was about to begin when the chanting grew louder, objects began to bounce off the windows, and there was repeated banging on the door.

"Let us stay calm and do as Robert suggested: call upon the loving protection and intervention of the Angels," said James.

Outside, there was an immediate flash of light across the night sky and then the appearance of what one of the sign-holders called a 'buzz being" - slivers of light that whirled and even sounded like a mini-tornado. Then all was calm – with several people later reporting that they stopped their protest in order to chat with someone they later described on television as 'the friendliest, nicest person you ever want to meet". Apparently he kept asking them what they "wanted to do or announce, what they now needed to create and contribute – for their own development and that of the community?"

And many who had thrown stones and fruit, now had their hands open, palms up and were acting as if they were conveying something to the person next to them. The newspaper quoted one of the participants

as saying, "It was not stones or even notes that we began to convey – but what some new and very magnetic person called 'pure, healing energy'."

Meanwhile, the rest of the crowd – including the hard-core instigators of the protest - had retreated to the bridge near the corner and were about to cross it. Apparently they were intent on escaping, determined to fight another day - when a very large figure stepped from shadows of one of the towers that supported the bridge. He held a long lance or spear that stood as high as his shoulder. His famous sword was also at side – ready for instant use. The area glowed with the radiance of His emerald green wings.

The lance vibrated and hummed as Michael raised it with both hands. He pointed it directly at the crowd - casting a steady beam of white light on their frozen faces. The image seemed to magnify and multiple, creating the sense that they were facing tens of giant angels - each armed with a long golden spear. The crowd halted – literally in their tracks. Stunned, they threw down their clubs, turned, and hurried away – each one scattering in a different direction.

The Gifted One

The camp of refugees was alive with activity when she arrived.

Trucks were unloading large crates filled with bottles of water, and the rumor was spreading that there would soon be a food drop – when the planes arrived with packages from the United Nations.

Dagney was helping to set up a hospital on the edge of the compound – the first for this particular camp of 3,500 refugees in western Somalia who were forced from their homes by the chaos created by that nation's civil war.

She had been here many times before – and always lent an immediate hand to whatever was in process. She had come to be known as the

'gifted one' for – unbeknownst to the rational part of her – she was able to give injections, change bandages, set broken bones, and always arrive with fresh supplies of something – usually coveted essentials like disinfectant, needles and thread, warm socks, children's clothing and bolts of cloth to make simple garments.

"The image seemed to magnify and multiple, creating the sense that they were facing tens of giant angels - each armed with a long golden spear."

Of course, the residents never saw her sleep — although exhaustion often forced her to rest. She simply showed up early on any given morning — at some unpredictable portion of the camp. Then by evening, she would seemingly vanish; turned the corner and was gone. "I am needed elsewhere," she would say, invariable adding: "But I will be back very soon - I assure you. In the meantime, I will be looking for batteries for the machines and duct tape to mend the plastic sheeting of the tents."

What they did not know, and what even Dagney could not fully explain, was that it was her out-of-body Soul that operated in Darfur — and now periodically in Haiti as well - while her physical body lay asleep in Manhattan. When the African evening arrived, or the fresh dawn in Haiti, her Soul would return to her home setting - where her body and mind were needed to get her daughter off to school and herself to work.

Dagney first encountered her Guardian Angel after Dagney's prayers had encouraged Sarah to leave the cloud she was sharing with Antonio and come to her aid. At the time, Dagney was still in a relationship with Jack and working at a downtown deli. Not any more. Dagney realized that the next three - or thirty years - with Jack were not likely to change anything in their partially convenient but really destructive relationship. It was not that it was so bad but that there was nothing really good about it. A long conversation, a repeat on the phone, the final surrender of the keys at the local restaurant — and Dagney was breathing free once again.

Her job and lifestyle were fine but they were not enough to sustain her physically or mentally. So she switched to part time (which fortunately included the bigger tips from the luncheon crowd), invested a major portion of her savings, and enrolled in nursing school. She would graduate in three, maybe four years; not bad. She had already spent that much time on Jack! At least she now had a future she could anticipate, one that would be much better for both her pocketbook and her sense of contribution and identity.

Besides, her morning memories were making her more and more aware – and appreciative - of her evening junkets, and that alone made life more meaningful and gratifying.

Then there was also the continuing presence of her wondrous Guardian Angel. The decision to return nightly to various refugee camps was Dagney's decision, yet Sarah was now always there as well. Often she would find the needed supplies and tucked them under Dagney's arm as she reentered the compound. Sarah also encouraged Dagney to trust herself, to take risks, to combine her intuition, wit and organizational skills to resolve any difficulty she encountered. Often she was also at Dagney's side, working along with her, infusing her with the healing energy that Dagney in turn transmitted to her patients.

What a Coincidence

And so it was that James finally met Dagney. First it was at the deli – a chance meeting at the end of her shift. She needed lunch before leaving and he needed somewhere to sit. So like good city folk they agreed to share the last table – then a double order of corn beef on rye with mustard and coleslaw. An easy exchange, some banter and lots of laughter led to some sharing about past and future. When they parted, the feeling was mutual: "*nice, really nice.*"

They met again 'by coincidence' two months later at Manhattan General. James was in the city, staying with his cousin for the weekend. He sprained his hand, went looking for a physical therapist, needed to sign in – and there was Dagney - who only the week before had started with the PT department as part of her in-service training.

A surprised and happy exchange of 'hi, how *are you?*', was followed by a scheduled lunch, then an evening movie, and in subsequent weeks, a Broadway play, a dinner, an invite, an embrace – and suddenly Dagney was juggling job, school, family and a relationship.

James by then was learning how to balance his new job as a techie for a library system, his continuing work with the healing community, and the essentials of courtship – which included getting to Dagney's apartment every other weekend (via train and subway), making himself scarce when Dagney 'really' needed to study, and mastering the games loved by her children.

In was not long, of course, before James and Dagney began to share stories of what they called "their spiritual encounters." Haiti and the refugees, the monastery and the monk; Sarah and Antonio, the nursing in Africa and the healing sessions in a church basement: different venues and approaches but each set of experiences revolving around the same essential focus.

Inevitably their meetings multiplied – by mutual desire and consent. Now they met – occasionally during the week and every weekend (or most of them) – sometimes at Dagney's but often she would now join James at the Church for the healing sessions. And come nightfall – on any day of the week – the two frequently convened in Somalia or in the Caribbean - or some comparable setting where the twosome focused on the needs of the refugee populations.

Often, in the morning after such joint ventures, the couple would invariably share again – in person, by phone or via e-mail depending on their locale. The healing sessions at the Sanctuary were easier to debrief but were also getting more difficult to coordinate since other places of worship were now asking for advise on how to set up similar programs.

As to the night travel, neither remembered any full accounts. But the glimpses recalled by one would invariably stir the recollections of the other, and bit-by-bit they would recapture enough clues and images to piece their stories together.

"I recall entering a series of tents." "Was that similar to what happened in your dream?" "There was also a sand storm." "We were sur-

rounded by armed militia." "Rows and rows of the suffering." "Then the healing began." "We were cooking food in large earthen pots." "We even found camels to transport the food." "Yes – I remember, we were together - transporting the food onto the camels!"

"And – despite the hard work under very difficult conditions, there always seemed to be extra energy available," said James. "The name Antonio keeps coming through. He calls them 'fly-bys': 'just checking to see if you need anything,' he would say. 'Please call whenever you need assistance. It is my mission to help you – so do not hesitate.'"

"Yes, yes, yes," Dagney would respond with great enthusiasm. "Sara – no I think it is spelled S-a-r-a-h. Her name keeps popping up in something I might be reading in a magazine or in a reference I randomly hear from across the hall. And 'presence' is her mode of participation. Your guy is there *in* an instant. My spirit helper never seems to leave *for* an instant. Same thing I suppose! I wonder if they know each other?"

The Grand Gathering

Ah, little do the Earthling know that the Angels are as sociable as they are. And in the angelic realm, there are no trains to catch, no conflicting schedules to coordinate, no babysitters to arrange, no chance meetings needed to close any emotional gap.

The entire host of angels – whatever one's stripe, mission, capacity or status – is joined at the hip when it comes to communicating, appreciating one another and expressing the deepest possible love of Prime Source. Talk about a high-key, incessant and everlasting love affair. That about summarizes the most dominant activity of the spiritual realm.

Here's Sarah and Antonio, for example – on that cloudlike perch of theirs.

"Dagney and James look good together, don't they?"

"And their work together is totally in synch - in body and out."

"And they really do call when they need assistance."

"And we love to fly by when we sense there is a cumulative need!"

"Oh: look who's en route – there to the left."

"I have one pendant with me," said Gabriel. "Here's Raphael with the other. And there - Michael is also about to arrive; He wanted to join the festivities too. He has to be very serious most of the time – the nature of his work does tend to reinforce his general disposition - so he also loves 'a night out' once in a while, as the humans say. He may even surprise us with an occasional twinkle and even a smile."

Gabriel allowed the combined shimmering of the august threesome to quiet down before making a formal announcement.

"Welcome everyone. As to the focus or our gathering," said Gabriel, we each and all want to congratulate both of you. You Antonio, and you Sarah, are no longer 'Guardian Angels in Training'. You are now full-fledged, full-time, bone fide 'Guardian Angels'!

"Prime Source asked us to tell you how delighted He is with the work you are doing – in particular with Dagney and James: 'smooth, delightful, loving and beautifully paced' is how he described it. Watch out: keep up this kind of work and you are sure to get many more assignments!"

A Full House

Suddenly they heard the sound of a soft 'swoooo-sh'. Then a slightly more pronounced, 'Vroom'.

It was Dagney, then James.

"We noticed that you had gathered, and then picked up on your conversation. So we wanted to stop by and thank all of you for helping us learn how to assist others," said Dagney.

"And to think our most immediate teachers were Guardian Angels – initially in training - and now full fledged," added James. "And their teachers – and our inspirations and guides as well – were a trio of eminent Archangels. Amazing. And there we were in our earthly settings having difficulty negotiating lives that centered on a diner and a deli."

"But we also wanted to tell you that our service – now around the globe - has really taken off – thanks to all of you," said Dagney. "We raise money in New York and now take the goodies and our selves to a series of sanctuaries and refugee camps - both in-body during the day and as itinerant Souls at night," she said smiling.

"And Dagney is a whiz at handling most of the organizational stuff – and already coordinates several corps of healers and nurses - in three countries," said James. "And I now have additional schools of healing arts, one in Haiti and two others in Africa. We both are also learning Haitian and African approaches to both community building and healing. It is all very powerful stuff."

"So we have all gained substantially," said Antonio. "You and your work, we and our badges, and our beloved Archangels doing what they do best, namely teaching, guiding and protecting all of us."

"Ah, but we sense we have the best combinations - in more ways than one," said James. "Corn beef is hard to come by in heaven, or on a cloud, and the kind of bodily hugs that young children, one's mate and the Africans and Haitians give so readily – are rare in any other realm. We definitely have the best of both worlds – and are we ever so thankful!"

The Ultimate Blessing

Just then came a thunderous roar and a bolt of lightning shook the cloud on which the group was gathered. It was followed by peals of hearty laughter.

"Greetings my wondrous partners!"

"Our sacred universe has not been created in a day – or a week," said the Voice. "Rather creation continues everyday, and each of you have contributed mightily to the process of love always seeking one more expression and form."

"I am particularly pleased, however, with what has been created *this* day," said Prime Source. "In fact, I am absolutely delighted with what - all of you, working as partners - have wrought. So I too wanted to join you in this joyful celebration – for such gatherings and displays of mutual support are an essential part of the great unfolding."

"Let us give thanks, then," She said, spreading Her hand over the entire group, "to one another, and for one another. May it always be Our abiding commitment - to never rest - from creating such camaraderie - and love - as this."

"And to mark the occasion," She added with a smile that spread throughout the Kosmos: "Henceforth, all of Us have ample reason to consider orange juice and the caduceus, as well as delis and shared tables - to be among our most loving symbols and activities."

Opportunities and Invitations

Do any of these sample encounters with the spiritual universe sound or feel familiar? Has anything like them ever happened to you? Do you remember having been in any similar situations or interacted with any of the spiritual entities or dimensions experienced by our wonderful cast of characters?

If so, do you recall who and/or what was involved, when it transpired, where it took place, approximately how long it took, and whether or not it has been repeated?

Suppose, however, that you have not yet had such an experience – or it was so long ago or so vague, indefinable and fleeting that you cannot recall any specifics. If so, then please consider the range of alternatives outlined here to be invitations – invitations to open your self to similar possibilities. It is a fascinating and incredibly supportive universe *out there* as well as *in here*. Could it be that habit keeps each of us from affirming our involvements or opening ourselves to the universe we have long sensed lies just beyond the thin veil of hesitation and tradition?

Remember all of our characters were so-called ordinary people until they allowed themselves to experience their extra-ordinary sensibilities. In an instant, what was formerly supra-ordinary can become an everyday reality to anyone who lays claim to their spiritual identity. And the transit to and from the mundane to the epic, the material to the spiritual - becomes much easier when explored and shared with other Kindred Spirits.

The spiritual realms have always been accessible to the mystics of all the religious traditions – which is why mystics are still universally both loved and admired. But direct entree to God bypasses the established intermediaries – institutional, clerical and ritual – and thus can be mighty threatening to established ways of thinking and entrenched ways of honoring the divine. Claiming a natural right and capacity

to communicate directly with God would inevitably lead to another radical redistribution of reverence and power.

If – as an immortal Soul – you possess the same innate constitution as your favorite mystic – then you can access your supra-ordinary powers by simply honoring your divine status. If and when you do so, be sure to simultaneously affirm your love of God and invoke His/Her/Its loving guidance and protection. Then be both trusting and patient. Spirit has a way of doing what is best for us – but on a timetable that serves the interest of our Soul – not our impatient ego.

It is also best to set some boundaries on your receptivity. There are some entities in the universe at-large – as it true right here on Earth - that may not have your best interests at heart. So it is very right and proper to tell such entities very emphatically that they are not invited, that your boundaries are sealed to their influence, and are open only to the counsel the of loving spirits who have your best interests at heart.

And please remember the moral of the last story in our trilogy, the one featuring *Angels*: do not allow your Guardian Angel to go unemployed much longer. Such a loving and enlightened being cannot honor – no less respond to - requests that you have long tended to keep to yourself.

So speak up. Remember, spirituality is a partnership with the divine. It takes two to complete any interaction no less a genuine and spirited tango, polka or foxtrot. And your loving partner, the one who has been waiting for you to declare yourself, is the same One you have long yearned to embrace.

The Author

William Francis Sturner, Ph.D., is the author of eleven books, father of two children, playmate of six grandchildren, lover of art and music, international consultant and facilitator, psychotherapist, and very spirited and joyful facilitator.

His work combines the perspective of growing up in the Bronx with the disciplines of Jungian, Gestalt and spiritual psychology. His university appointments have included full professorships at three American universities and vice presidencies at two. He has also been awarded visiting appointments at the universities of Limerick, Istanbul Technical, Buffalo State, Santiago de Compostela and Moscow State.

He has offered workshops and consulting throughout the USA, Europe, the Middle East, Africa and Latin America, and is a regular presenter at international conferences on Creativity and Innovation.

He lives in East Aurora, NY at his 'Open Heart Sanctuary' – fourteen acres of woods, ponds and trails - on which he has constructed a 54' Chartres Labyrinth, a Hobbit House, and a series of large environmental sculptures.

wfsturner@mac.com

www.KindredSpirits.Us

Made in the USA
Charleston, SC
04 April 2011